To our good neighbors and true friends,
Curley and Doris Lee,
in appreciation of who and what they are

LEGACY OF SILVER

LEGACY OF SILVER

Colleen L. Reece

CHIVERS

British Library Cataloguing in Publication Data available

Published in 2004 in the U.K. by arrangement with the Author.

U.K. Hardcover ISBN 0-7540-9922-9
U.K. Softcover   ISBN 0-7540-9923-7

The text of this Large Print edition is unabridged.
Other aspects of the book may vary from the original edition.

Set in 16 pt. New Times Roman.

Printed in Great Britain on acid-free paper.

British Library Cataloguing in Publication Data available

Printed and bound in Great Britain by
Antony Rowe Ltd., Chippenham, Wiltshire

1

Silver Trevelyan lightly touched the flanks of her horse. "Go, Sultan!"

Powerful muscles rippled under the shining black skin as he responded. A leap, then a steady gallop, left Silver's friend Lucy Anne Simmons on her horse, Calico, far behind.

Silver allowed him to run free, leaning forward over his neck, calling in his ear. Her hat disappeared somewhere behind him, followed moments later by hairpins, and her black hair, dark as her laughing velvet eyes, tumbled free.

Gradually she reined the horse in. "All right, Sultan. Enough for today." He slowed to a canter, then a trot, and at last paused near the edge of the grassy rise overlooking Silver Birches.

"Come on, Lucy Anne!" Silver beckoned imperiously, waving a riding crop she never used.

Lucy Anne's hail preceded her more cautious approach. Silver vainly attempted to gather her black hair into some semblance of order, noting how meticulous Lucy Anne looked. Small, dainty, with trusting brown eyes that matched her chestnut waves, Lucy Anne never got mussed, even when riding. In spite of her love for the younger girl, Silver sighed. Sometimes she felt like a splashy oil painting next to a delicate watercolor when Lucy Anne visited.

Her disloyal thought was swallowed up in genuine affection for Lucy Anne. "Wasn't that a grand race?"

Wild-rose pink stained the smooth cheeks. With more than her usual spunk, Lucy Anne retorted, "Some race! Calico isn't known for her speed."

"Want to ride Sultan?" Silver offered wickedly.

"Don't be absurd." Lucy Anne slid from the saddle and looked up at Silver. "You should see yourself! Hair mussed, eyes blazin', even your magnolia-white skin's red as a holly berry!" Yet only admiration shone in the gentle face.

"I know." Silver slid to the ground and let Sultan's reins hang. "Everyone says now that I'm goin' to be twenty-one I have to act it." She flung herself next to Lucy Anne defiantly. "Why do we have to grow up, anyway? So what if I'm twenty-one tomorrow? Just because I'm not married and havin' babies, am I a freak, or somethin'?"

"You're no freak." Lucy Anne's frankness

had the effect of cold water on a hot fire. "It's just because you're Silver Trevelyan, heiress to all this —" She waved to the rolling expanses before them. "The whole state of Virginia knows about Colonel Leigh's Silver Birches plantation."

The fire in Silver's eyes was temporarily quenched, and her gaze followed Lucy Anne's pointing finger. Over the rise where they sat, Trevelyan land stretched forever, it seemed. As far as they could see, all belonged to Silver Trevelyan's grandfather and would one day be hers. Negroes in the tobacco fields, the three-story house with white columns pointing to heaven, quarters for the slaves, orchards, and barns, Silver Birches filled the valley between the hills — and more. Even the small river winding through like a silver ribbon lay on Trevelyan land.

Silver threw back her head in sheer happiness. Her dark eyes drank it all in. "I could come here a hundred times a day and never tire of it. It's so beautiful and peaceful! I don't ever want to leave it."

"You won't have to, if Taylor Randolph has anything to say about it," Lucy Anne teased.

She was rewarded with a hot blush that turned Silver's face even more scarlet.

"Now you're the one who's bein' absurd. He's years older than I am. Can you imagine me ever gettin' spoony with him?"

"You have to marry someone." Lucy Anne was always practical. "You'll need a strong man to manage this place."

Silver fired up again. "I can run it myself, if I have to. I won't." Her eyes fixed unseeingly on the dark cloud that had appeared at the far edge of the blue horizon, topping a slight hill and growing with every movement of the early April wind. "Someday someone will come ridin' across the mountains. . . ."

Lucy Anne's twinkling brown eyes opened wide. "Why, Silver, I never suspected you were so romantic!"

Silver shook herself, disgusted for letting Lucy Anne peep inside her feelings, even for a moment. "Forget what I said. I just don't aim to marry Taylor Randolph, even if he does have the second-biggest place in these parts." She swung back toward Lucy Anne. "Why all this talk of marryin'? Has brother Frank been pesterin' you again?"

"He doesn't pester." The muffled words escaped white-gloved fingers suddenly pressed over burning-hot cheeks.

Silver regretted her thrust and hastily made amends. "He really is in love with you, Lucy Anne. He has been ever since your father brought you over to get acquainted, when you were ten years old. There's never been anyone else for Frank, wild Indian that he sometimes acts."

"Seven years ago." Lucy Anne ticked them off on her fingers. "Mama had just died and your father. Maybe that's why we've always been so close." A slight frown crossed her face. "I don't remember much about Mama, except she cried a lot. She wasn't well for a long time before she died." A breeze lifted a strand of her shining hair. "Do you remember your father — a lot, I mean?"

"Yes," Silver said, "but then, I was fourteen. He was so different from the colonel! His name was Blair, and he was a dreamer, the colonel says. He loved hunting and riding and entertainin', but he loved books even more. The colonel says there's too much of Father in Frank for Frank to ever be a good plantation owner! That's why he's breakin' every tradition and leavin' Silver Birches to me." Silver made a face. "As soon as it's actually mine, I'm havin' papers made so half goes to Frank." The teasing light came back in her face. "And to you."

"Funny how you always call your grandfather 'the colonel.' "

"Can you imagine me ever callin' him

'Granddaddy'?" Silver's laugh pealed over the valley below and was echoed in Lucy Anne's soft laugh. "Lucy Anne, I don't mean to pry, but — you do care for Frank, don't you?"

"With all my heart." The fervent answer brought more color to her thin face, but her brown eyes met Silver's steadily. "He's everthin' I've ever dreamed about, all my picture-book heroes in one."

Silver drew a quick breath. She couldn't see Frank in such a role, but then, she was his sister. What about him had captured Lucy Anne's love and held it from the time he was twelve until now?

"I can hardly wait until you're really my sister!" Her impulsive words coaxed Lucy Anne's lips into a smile. "I just don't understand, though. If you and Frank truly love each other, why aren't you already married?"

Lucy Anne's shoulders drooped. "I don't know. Frank spoke to Father a long time ago, but Father says I'm too young."

"Too young! When half the girls in the countryside are married between fourteen and sixteen?" Silver indignantly refuted Mr. Simmons's reasoning. "Seems like you're old enough, if it's what you want."

"There's something strange about it,

Silver." Lucy Anne leaned forward, her confidence low. "I don't know what it is, but every time anythin' is said about my marryin', Father changes the subject. He just says, 'You're too young to be settin' up housekeepin',' and won't say more." Her questioning glance intrigued Silver. "Maybe he promised Mama somethin', or maybe he knows a secret. He barely talks about Mama anymore." Horror from a new thought clouded her eyes. "What if — if there's insanity in my background?"

Fear clutched Silver's throat, but she thrust it aside. "Now you are being ridiculous! You're as sane as I am. Although —" She laughed. "Some might tell you that's no compliment!"

Her little ruse worked. Lucy Anne's white face returned to normal color. "Well, there's somethin' more than my age." She sighed. "I suppose I'll find out when it's time."

Silver impetuously jumped up. "Let's talk about somethin' else. Did you know Mammy finished my gown for my birthday party tomorrow night? It's the grandest I've ever had. It's bluer than peacock feathers and shinier than Sultan when he's brushed." She patted her horse. "You should have seen the dressmaker, when I picked out the blue. 'My dear,' " her voice was a perfect imitation of the wispy woman who handled her wardrobe. " 'Brunettes *do not* wear that shade of blue! You should choose pink or yellow.' I laughed and told her I had a wardrobe full of pink and yellow gowns, and I intended to have the blue. After I held the fabric up next to my face, she gave in."

A ripple of laughter escaped Silver at the memory of the good woman's face. "I couldn't help addin' that if she thought the blue unsuitable, I'd have the scarlet material we saw in a window in Lynchburg."

"You didn't!" Lucy Anne's horrified gasp delighted Silver.

"Of course I did. I wanted to see what she'd say. She pursed up her lips and stuck her nose in the air. 'No *lady* wears red, miss.' " Her mimicry sent Lucy Anne into gales of laughter. "I wouldn't, really, since people say what they do about girls who wear red, but I just had to get her mind off how unsuitable the blue was."

"You sure know how to get your own way."

"Why not?" Silver stretched, a small smile creeping over her lips. "If I'm Silver Trevelyan of Silver Birches, there's no reason I shouldn't have what I want. I'll wear that blue gown, and Virginia will long remember my twenty-first birthday." She stopped and caught up a small stick. "See? I'll even put it in the ground of Silver Birches." She dug the stick in the soft earth and carved: *April 12, 1861.*

"Will Frank be home in time?"

"He promised." Silver straightened and threw away the stick. "He's been visitin' in Lynchburg and will ride home tomorrow."

"But that's forty miles." Lucy Anne's anxiety reflected in her comment.

"Nothin' will stop Frank, when he makes up his mind. Besides, he promised to bring me a surprise." Twin dimples flashed in her cheeks. "I can't imagine what it is! He said it's big and red and green and tan, and I'm bound to love it. He said it might even arrive before he did."

"Whatever can fit that description?" Lucy Anne wondered.

"I don't know, but I get all shivery, thinkin' about it." Silver reluctantly turned toward Sultan. "I hate leavin' here; it's so peaceful. I'm so glad you're goin' to spend a week with me! I wouldn't have had you miss my birthday ball for anythin'."

Lucy Anne slowly stood, watching the storm cloud across the valley. It had increased until it filled a good portion of the southern sky. "Silver, that storm cloud makes me afraid. Do you think there's goin' to be war?"

A sharp twinge shot through Silver even as she scoffed, "Here? Of course not!" Her indignation grew. "Why'd you ever bring up such a thing, Lucy Anne Simmons?"

"I've been scared ever since all those states left the Union and set up their own Confederate States of America," Lucy Anne confessed. "First South Carolina, last December, then within six weeks, Alabama, Mississippi, Louisiana, Florida, Georgia, and Texas."

"Don't blame them a bit!" Silver lashed at her boot with her riding crop and succeeded in stirring up dust. "Why should a bunch of Yankees tell us how to live?" Memory of the colonel's views on the subject inflamed Silver's answer. "They are just jealous because the South's rich! They holler about slaves, but they have Negroes workin' in their own kitchens."

"I just don't see how some of the states can secede." Lucy Anne's troubled eyes were pools of doubt. "Isn't it kind of as if an arm says it won't be part of the body anymore? It's still part of the body. It can't just separate itself."

"Why should we worry about it? Those

states are a long way from here. Let them do what they want. We're 'way over here between Lynchburg and Lexington. No one's goin' to make war on us!"

"We can't be sure, Silver." Lucy Anne looked away from her and across the valley. "Father says Virginia may have to choose whether to join the Confederate States or stay with the Union." She took a deep, ragged breath. "If war comes, Frank will go, and Taylor Randolph, and every young man around."

Silver impatiently mounted Sultan and caught up the reins. "You are a real goose, Lucy Anne. There isn't goin' to be any war! At least not here. Why, no one in the world would want to declare war and bother this valley!" She gestured across the suddenly still landscape, checkered by swiftly moving clouds. "It's all just a political thing and won't amount to a hill of beans."

Lucy Anne was staring at the growing clouds. "That's how the storm that's comin' started, too. Now look at it." A large drop of rain splattered the dusty earth where they'd been sitting. "Even our horses are nervous. They can feel it comin'." Her pinched face mirrored the gray skies above. "I'm really scared, Silver." One hand reached blindly for support.

Silver shuddered. For a moment the weirdly racing clouds had cast an ominous shadow over her natural joy of living. She forced a laugh and clasped Lucy Anne's hand. "Let's go home. When we get inside, we can laugh over this stormy day and curl up in front of the fireplace in my room. We're goin' to get soaked, if we don't hurry."

Another large drop hit with driving force. Sultan snorted and pranced nervously. "Go ahead with Calico, Lucy Anne. Sultan and I will follow. Now go!"

Lucy Anne clambered aboard Calico and headed back the way they had come. The shortcut trail down the side of the rise would save time but, if it rained hard, it would be slippery. Had Silver been alone, she might have chanced it. Outrunning a storm with Sultan was one of her greatest joys. To laugh and shake her fist in the face of nature was to conquer.

Now she sighed. Lucy Anne and the storm had managed to take the fine edge off her anticipation of her birthday. Why did everyone have to be so concerned with war, anyway? Wasn't it enough to live at Silver Birches and oversee all the things that had to be tended? All this talk of freeing the slaves was nonsense. Where would they go?

Mammy, for example. If she were freed, she'd probably roll her big dark eyes and say, 'What fo' you free me? I'se ben watchin' Miss Silver ever since she be born. I'se goin' right on doin' what I ben doin', and that's all ther is to it.' "

Silver thought of the neat cabins housing their own slaves. No one of them was ever mistreated. Colonel Trevelyan was strict but almost fanatical on that point. He'd horsewhipped an overseer for beating a farm hand. A wave of pride swept through Silver. The colonel was the finest man she knew, now that Father was gone. Tall, erect in spite of his years, shoulders back in the military way he'd kept from fighting in the War of 1812, he was all a plantation owner should be.

"We've been given much," he was fond of saying. "Now it's our responsibility before Almighty God to take care of it." Never a day ended without the colonel reading from the old Bible in the small family sitting room. Even balls and parties were not allowed to interfere. He managed to slip away for at least a few minutes and expected his family to do the same. Silver could recall impatiently waiting for him to finish reading while her toe tapped in time to only partially muted music, then rushing back to her partners to make up for time that seemed lost.

If only all the plantation owners treated their slaves the way the colonel does, there would be no trouble, Silver thought passionately. She'd heard Taylor Randolph whipped his slaves if they did anything wrong. There had been tales of his selling a female slave who'd been married to one of his field hands. She never knew why; it was hushed up when she came in the room. Maybe that was the reason she shrank from his bold courtship and avoided being alone with him. Her tender heart could not bear cruelty. In this she was like Frank.

Watching Lucy Anne through the steadily growing rain, another rush of love filled her. If only Mr. Simmons would agree to Lucy Anne's marrying Frank! Her laughing, dark-eyed, dark-haired brother, who was a tall replica of herself, would cherish Lucy Anne always.

A stab of envy filled her. How wonderful it must be to be so sure of yourself, so filled with the knowledge there was only one person to bring happiness. Would such love ever seek her out? Depression fell over her like one of the black clouds above, dumping its contents. Tomorrow she would be twenty-one years old, far older than most girls when they married. Some of her friends already had four- and five-year-old miniatures of themselves, chattering away. She loved children. Someday she hoped for a son who would look like his father and a daughter like herself.

She closed her eyes, letting Sultan pick his sure way toward home. Good thing she'd found her hat, although if it continued to rain the way it was now, she'd still be soaked. It took hours to dry her hair. If she dared, she'd cut it into a short, curly mass that would be easier to care for.

Thought of herself with short curls lightened her mood. How everyone would stare! Yet she couldn't give up her beautiful hair. Even Mammy said it was her crowning glory, the wealth of hair that became so inconvenient when she rode.

The trail widened into a road, and she caught up with Lucy Anne. The younger girl's brown hair curled riotously beneath her hat. Her eyes no longer held storm clouds, but regret. "I'm sorry if I spoiled your day." Her mobile lips quivered.

How sensitive she is! Silver thought. "It's all right. Lucy Anne, guess what I was just thinkin'?"

Lucy Anne's troubles dissolved. "I can never guess what you are thinkin'!"

"I was wonderin' how it would feel to get

my hair cut so it was just short curls. It sure would be easier to take care of when I'm outdoors."

"You wouldn't!" If Lucy Anne had been aghast at Silver's notion of wearing red to the ball, she was appalled at this new suggestion. "Promise me you'll never cut it! It'd be just like you to do somethin' outlandish like that to show everyone you're your own boss."

Silver's eyes gleamed. "I might at that."

"Promise me you won't, ever!" Lucy Anne was taking no chances.

"Not unless it's to save my life!" Silver laughed outright at the shock in Lucy Anne's face. "I'm too vain to cut off my 'crownin' glory.' Even if the temptation is there."

They had reached the great white mansion. "Here, boy." Silver threw Sultan's reins to the waiting stable boy.

"Come on, Lucy Anne. I may shock you to death, but I don't intend you to catch your death from dampness." She led the way into the great hall and stood dripping on the polished floor. "Mammy will see that our clothes are dried. Besides, your trunk will be unpacked by now. I told her to put you in my room." She smiled and led the way up the carved white staircase leading to the upper levels. Brocaded walls and price-less paintings hung everywhere, lending an aura of opulence to the hall. Doors led off to other rooms: the great library, family sitting room, and ballroom.

Silver turned to smile over her shoulder at Lucy Anne. She rounded the right-angle curve leading to her own suite — and failed to see the person striding down the hall. Their crash was inevitable. The next instant Silver lay on the richly carpeted floor, looking miles into the air at the tallest man she had ever seen, whose flaming red hair and concerned green eyes stood out in sharp contrast to his highly tanned face.

All red and green and tan and big, and you're bound to love it. It may even arrive before I do. Was the giant helping her to her feet Frank's birthday surprise? The thought struck her dumb. Wait until she got her hands on her miserable brother!

2

"Why, miss!" Even in her speechless state, Silver noted the crispness of the words, free from the soft southern slur she was accustomed to hearing. Lucy Anne's soft giggle didn't help matters.

"I'm a clumsy oaf." The giant managed to get Silver and her bedraggled garments upright. "You aren't hurt, are you?"

Silver mutely shook her head. Something seemed to have happened to her power of speech.

"It's just that I was in such a hurry to see Silver —"

Speech returned with a rush. "You wish to see Silver?" How dared this stranger barge in like this, knock her down, then refer to her as other than *Miss Trevelyan?*

Shaggy eyebrows raised at the disdain in her voice. "Of course. Tomorrow's her birthday, isn't it?" He picked up the box he'd dropped when they collided and held it out. "Frank asked me to stay over for her party. He said his little sister would be pleased. Do you think Silver will like my gift?"

Silver's eyes involuntarily dropped to the

open box. The largest doll she had ever seen, dressed in French fashion, stared up at her with knowing brown eyes.

A rush of pride and humiliation roared through her, but before she could wither the stranger with a glance, Lucy Anne came out of her openmouthed trance and said, "She ought to love it. One thin', though —" She ignored Silver's gasp. "We all call her Miss Trevelyan until we get to know her extremely well. She's a mighty important person around here." She gave Silver a wicked wink.

The stranger laughed aloud. "Oh, she won't mind if I call her Silver." The assurance in his easy laugh sent prickles of rage through Silver. "Frank's told me so much about her I feel I already probably know her better than she knows herself."

Silver's tongue loosened. "Oh, you do, do you! Well, let me tell you somethin', Mr. Whoever-you-are. I am *Miss* Silver Trevelyan, and you and your stupid doll can go back wherever you came from." She swept past him as haughtily as she could, her performance somewhat marred by trickles of water from her long, wet skirts, which left puddles on the polished floorboards and soaked into the Persian runner.

If she had expected stricken silence, she

was doomed to disappointment. As she entered her own room, head high and followed by the helplessly giggling Lucy Anne, she heard a great shout of laughter and a quiet voice, "So *that's* Frank Trevelyan's little sister!" and another burst of laughter. Silver's eyes snapped, and she slammed the door to relieve her feelings. But the heavy door didn't shut, because of the thick carpet.

"Silver, I've never seen you so —" Lucy Anne fell into a settee and completely dissolved. Her shoulders shook. Her hat fell off, and her face ran tears from her mirth.

"Stop it, Lucy Anne!" Silver whirled from the middle of the room. "Of all the arrogant, overbearin', obnoxious —"

"Handsome," Lucy Anne supplied, coming upright and mopping her sparkling face.

"Handsome!" Silver's scornful repetition of the word only set Lucy Anne off again.

"He really is all red and green and tan." Lucy Anne fluttered her lashes. "And Frank says you just can't help lovin' him."

"Love him?" Silver could feel anger creep from her toes, warming her rain-soaked body and sending red flags into her face. "Not if he were the last man on earth. I could never, never love a creature like that!"

Lucy Anne tittered, and Silver followed her stare, turning back to the partly open door.

"*Never* is a long time, Miss Trevelyan." The stranger stood in the opening. He tossed her dripping hat to a nearby table.

"Well, aren't you goin' to apologize?" Silver held her breath.

"Apologize? For what? It was an honest mistake." A little smile curved around the mobile lips, as if he were actually enjoying himself.

"Sir!" Every trace of color fled, leaving her pale. "You come bustin' into my home, unannounced —" A new thought widened her eyes. "Why, we don't even know who you are!"

"I had expected your brother to make proper introductions. However," he smiled again, revealing strong white teeth, "allow me. Miss Trevelyan, Miss —"

"Simmons," Lucy Anne put in.

"May I present myself? Zachary Stuart of Harmony, Virginia, very much at your service." He waited, but when he received no response, stepped toward the door. "If you will excuse me, ladies, I'll step down and introduce myself to the colonel. Oh, I almost forgot." He pulled the offensive doll box from behind him. "Perhaps you'd rather this didn't appear with your other gifts at the birthday ball." The next instant he was gone, closing the door behind him, with a firm hand.

"So that's Zach Stuart!"

"Why so awestruck?" Silver forced herself to stop staring at the door.

"Don't you know who he is?" Lucy Anne demanded.

"Never heard the name before." She began removing her clammy skirt.

"You should have." Every bit of merriment was gone. Lucy Anne's brown eyes shone. "He's the doctor who saved Frank's life a year ago, when Frank went to those races at Richmond."

It was Silver's turn to stare then drop to a chair, heedless of the mess she was making with her wet clothing. "Lucy Anne! It can't be. He said he was from Harmony."

"So maybe he went to a medical convention or somethin'," her friend said impatiently. "He's the one, anyway. I'll never forget Frank tellin' how he was pitchin' over King Blair's head and not wakin' up for three days, then findin' out Zach Stuart had stayed with him the whole time."

Silver's face shadowed. "I won't forget, either — but I don't remember ever hearin' the doctor's name."

Lucy Anne looked at her pityingly. "I reckon he has a right to make an honest mistake, Silver. If Frank told him you were his little sister, what else could he think?"

Generous as she was imperious, Silver rushed for the door. "I have to tell him I'm sorry. What if he leaves?"

"He won't." Lucy Anne cocked her head. "He isn't the kind of man who'll let a girl get ahead of him. Better wait till you're dressed before goin' after him."

The wisdom of Lucy Anne's words proved themselves when Silver caught a glimpse of herself in the great mirror above the bureau. "What a mess! It's a wonder he didn't think I was a Salem witch." She made a distasteful mouth and pulled a bell rope.

"I think you've met your match, Silver."

"Whatever do you mean?" Silver came out of a flurry of petticoats and caught sight of the twinkle in Lucy Anne's eyes.

"He sure isn't much like Taylor Randolph."

Hours later, Lucy Anne's laughing words intruded on the table small talk, commanding Silver's full attention. Although she had been seated next to Zach Stuart, she could see him clearly with her wide vision. Across the table Taylor Randolph's smooth blond hair gleamed in the light of candles that reflected in the polished table. His rather narrow eyes had scarcely left Silver since she entered. On the other hand, immaculately dressed Zach Stuart paid no more attention to Silver than if she had been a scarecrow imported to fill a space at the long table. He was deep in discussion with the colonel.

At least Silver could free herself from impatience and irritation by looking at her grandfather. Had there ever been a more shining example of the Virginia plantation owner than the colonel? Her heart swelled with pride. His silver hair shone even brighter than Taylor Randolph's. His blue eyes were wide and open, his face ruddy with good health. Advancing age had only speeded him up. He was invincible, a rock of strength that had supported Silver all the years of her life. How she loved him! He could be depended on to do right, to love and honor and cherish —

"Miss Trevelyan, may I have the pleasure of your company ridin' tomorrow?" Taylor's spectacular smile lingered as he held onto the last word.

"Why," Silver hesitated, and in the split second a crisp voice asked, "I'd hoped you'd be willing to show me about Silver

Birches, Miss Trevelyan. Your grandfather said you might."

Feeling reprieved, Silver smiled across at Taylor. "The colonel's word is law here, Mr. Randolph." She saw warning signals in his darkening eyes and hastened to add, "Don't forget you're to lead the ball's openin' dance with me tomorrow night." The storm warnings subsided, but Taylor gave Zach Stuart a look of pure hatred. "Besides," Silver rushed on, "I'll be busy makin' myself ready most of the day."

"I can't believe you need much time for that," Taylor said gallantly, but Zach didn't reply. Silver could feel an undercurrent even while dinner was finished and the men went to smoke, leaving the ladies to go ahead to the drawing room.

How could I see Dr. Stuart alone? Silver wondered. She had to apologize for her hasty words. Resentment mingled with gratitude swept through her. Even if he had saved Frank, he needn't have laughed at her. She hated being made to look ridiculous and knew she had come off second best in the little skirmish upstairs.

In a fever of dread and impatience, she waited, after the men joined them, obligingly playing for an hour on the spinet, then watching for a chance. There was none. She was on the verge of suggesting a stroll in the moonlight when the colonel looked at his ornately carved gold watch and said, "Bedtime, I believe. Tomorrow's a big day."

"Did you get to see Dr. Stuart?" Lucy Anne whispered as they swept up the stairs, long skirts trailing the now-scrubbed steps.

"No." Silver sounded peevish. "But I will tomorrow." She lowered her voice as Mammy came in to help the girls unfasten their gowns.

Yet long after Lucy Anne lay asleep, Silver's mind relived the crash on the stairs and the following encounter in her sitting room. How could Lucy Anne think he was handsome? He was too rugged and masculine to be considered good-looking. All that red hair and those inquiring green eyes weren't quite in good taste. She tossed restlessly. Hadn't he even noticed how the white dress caught up here and there with rosebuds showed off her soft shoulders and white arms? Taylor Randolph had noticed.

A shiver of revulsion went through her. More than ever she was determined never to marry Taylor. Ugh! He had looked as if he wanted to eat her. For the first time she had wished her gown was cut higher, although she never allowed the dressmaker to cut her clothes so low her bosom showed, as so many of her friends did. Even the cherished peacock-blue ball gown had a lacy undertrim that framed her shoulders and gave an air of modesty.

Her friends Sally Trenton and Mabel Grant laughed at her, but Silver didn't care. She was not going to expose herself as they did. But Taylor's almost-vulgar stare disturbed her.

She turned her thoughts to more pleasant things: the beautiful dress even now encased in muslin and hanging ready for the ball. Although the dressmaker made her gowns, Mammy jealously guarded the task of hand finishing each, adding tricks of trim and lace that set Silver's clothing apart from even the French gowns her friends wore. The colonel was death on imported gowns, one of the few things he adamantly insisted she observe. "Virginia's good enough for anyone," he maintained. "Get what you want of goods from England and the like, but they'll be made right here by Virginians."

Zach Stuart would be like that, too, she thought. Her lips curved in a smile. It would be interesting to see who would give way first, if they ever clashed!

Zach Stuart's introduction to Silver Birches was nearly over when Silver reined in her horse. Lucy Anne had already gone to the house, but Silver lingered. Now that she had the opportunity to speak, she was strangely shy. Finally she said, "I wish to apologize for my rudeness yesterday, Dr. Stuart."

"So you know who I am — now."

The inflection in his voice sent a wave of scarlet to her hair. "Yes. Will you be friends?" Why should she hold her breath? She'd never before felt this way about any of her other friends.

"Gladly!" His iron grip clasped her small, gloved hand, and he helped her dismount. "I'm afraid I was the one who acted rudely." He laughed his contagious laugh. "I really was expecting a little girl."

"I'll have Frank's head for his mischief," she exclaimed.

"Don't. We won't give him the satisfaction of knowing how well his trick almost worked." He frowned, green eyes turning to liquid emeralds. "Will Miss Simmons keep our little secret?"

"She had better!" Silver smiled at his ferocious look.

His face smoothed out. "You're saving some dances for me tonight, aren't you, Miss Trevelyan?"

Her old coquettishness returned. "Maybe

one, Dr. Stuart." She ran for the house, stopped, and glanced over her shoulder. He was still in the same spot, watching her. "Maybe even a second." She waved and turned toward the open door, nearly colliding with Taylor Randolph, who must have heard every word.

"What do you mean, playin' with that outsider?" He caught her arm.

His possessive tone roused fighting instincts in Silver. She jerked herself free. "I can't see that's any of your concern, sir."

"It's my concern when the woman I intend to marry flirts with every man who happens to come by." His eyes were murderous.

"I haven't said I'd marry you." *And I never will,* she almost added but restrained herself at the red glow in his eyes.

"You acted friendly enough until he came." Taylor nodded at Stuart, who was leading the horses away.

"More's the pity." Silver coldly turned away, refusing to look back when he called, "I never give up when I want somethin'. I get it — always."

The audacity of him! She burst into her room and startled Lucy Anne, who was preparing for a beauty nap. The story spilled out, and her friend looked serious. "He's not one to trifle with. He's better as a friend than an enemy."

"I thought Dr. Stuart was bold, but after this! I declare, these men are gettin' out of hand. Why can't they be like the colonel? I can't imagine him actin' so disrespectful."

"Be fair, Silver. Dr. Stuart really wasn't disrespectful, just more like a boy havin' fun." Lucy Anne's lips twitched.

Silver capitulated. "You're right." She flung herself down without even removing her boots. "I think he could be a good friend."

Lucy Anne changed the subject. "I wish Frank would come. Seems he would have left Lynchburg early, so he could be here by now."

"He'll be here," Silver said. "He promised."

Yet when they roused from their nap and asked Mammy, she shook her head. "No sign o' him, honey."

"He's probably goin' to dash in and make a grand entrance," Silver commented. "You know how Frank loves a good show."

Mammy served them a light supper in Silver's room. "Jes' so's you won't be a-stuffin' yo'selves in front o' comp'ny," she ordered. Silver was too excited to eat. Fresh from baths, clad in voluminous petticoats and chemises and pantaloons, she and Lucy Anne took turns having their hair dressed by Mammy, who'd become expert.

"Now for the dresses," Lucy Anne breathed. The rosy silk with black bands of velvet set her off perfectly. No need for surreptitious pinching of cheeks for extra color. Her face was aflame with excitement.

But Silver gasped as she saw her own reflection. Was it the new silhouette of flat in front, standing out behind, that gave the gown its elegance? Or the sheen of the silk? Or simply the daring color? Or was it something shining in the depths of her midnight-black eyes that made her more beautiful than ever before?

"You've never been lovelier." Lucy Anne's frank appraisal brought a little color to Silver's exquisite skin.

"Neither have you." Silver's eyes met Lucy Anne's in the mirror. "Think anyone else will be belle of the ball tonight?"

Lucy Anne's mouth quivered. "I just wish Frank would come." She pressed one hand over her heart. "Somethin' in here feels funny. I hope there's nothin' wrong."

Silver's well-hidden bump of anxiety grew, dimming her radiance a bit. Frank was wild, but she'd never known him to break a promise. Where could he be?

"Folks' a-comin'," mammy reminded, her broad face one large grin, teeth white as the turban above it. "You better be a-gittin'."

Carriages by the score, single horses, elegantly gowned women, some of whom had been on hand earlier and who had dressed in other rooms, converged on the great ballroom.

"The new French chandeliers barely got here in time," Silver confided. "There are almost a hundred candles in each one!"

Lucy Anne gasped. Every candle flame was magnified by the crystal surrounding it. Flames were further magnified in the highly polished dark floorboards, until the room was a whirl of light and laughter. "It's the most beautiful room I ever saw."

"It wasn't until I convinced the colonel that French chandeliers were not a Virginia product and had to be imported that he let me get them. You know how he is about Virginia!" Silver's eyes swept the great room. Cream walls, high ceilings, white columns holding up the great timbers, gilt trim — it truly was, as Lucy Anne had said, the most beautiful room possible. Even rooms in other plantations and some of the historic homes she'd visited boasted nothing lovelier.

"Where's that young whippersnapper brother of yours?" the colonel demanded, white brows nearly touching.

"He promised to be here."

"Hmph. Can't wait any longer. Already past time for the ball to be opened. You leadin' off with Taylor Randolph?"

Silver nodded.

"Good. He's a mighty fine man." Silver could see the satisfaction in her grandfather's face. "Don't you forget that, missy."

"How can I help it, when he keeps remindin' me?" she asked pertly, and he scowled and pushed her toward Taylor, resplendent in evening dress.

The ball flowed on. Yet as Silver was whirled from partner to partner, a gnawing disturbance grew inside. Frank ought to be there. He had promised, and it was her birthday. Her growing anxiety was reflected in Lucy Anne's brown eyes. Each time they met in a quadrille, the same unanswered question peered forth. Silver was on the point of seeking out the colonel and confessing her worry when Dr. Stuart claimed his first dance. "Miss Trevelyan, I believe this is mine?" He captured her from a laughing, protesting mob of admirers. But instead of leading her to the floor, he opened a French door and ushered her onto the cool porch outside. "Before we dance, I want you to know something. I made a vow I would never take in my arms any woman except the one I hoped to one day make my wife. I never have. My dancing will not be polished, although I have observed I can manage not to tread on your slippers and lovely gown."

So he was aware of her looks! Hard on the thought came full realization of what he had said, "Your wife!" She looked up at him. The light from the Chinese lanterns strung about the lawn dappled her face.

"Yes. I know it's too soon, but I'm leaving tomorrow. May I come back to call, someday — with your full knowledge of why I will come?"

Silver was saved from an answer by the staccato beat of horses' hooves. She ran to the steps. "Frank! Are you hurt? Where have you been?"

Her shrill cries pierced even the gaiety of the ballroom. Couples spilled out. Colonel Leigh Trevelyan strode to the yard, taking in the lathered horse and the half circle of sweat-stained men behind his grandson. "You know better than to ride a horse and half kill it! What's the meanin' of this tomfoolery?"

Frank was ashen. He tried twice to speak.

Silver felt Lucy Anne's fingers digging into her arm and heard her gasp at Frank's appearance. Was he *drunk?* And on her birthday?

"I demand you tell me what the meanin' of this is, young man!"

The cold order stopped the trembling of Frank's lips. He pulled himself together and slid to the ground, instinctively reaching out for the grandfather who had never understood him. "It's war, sir!"

Silver's heart stood still. Her eyes never left her brother's face.

"General Pierre Beauregard demanded the surrender of Fort Sumter. Major Anderson refused." Frank gulped and half sobbed. "Beauregard fired on Fort Sumter today."

The cloud Lucy Anne had seen suddenly became a thundercloud. The storm was upon them — and there was no escape.

3

Silver sagged against the column next to her, feeling Lucy Anne's fingers turn to steel and bite into her arm, but ignoring the pain. "War!" Her whisper was lost in the outcry of the crowd that had been happy such a short time before. Blank faces stared at the disheveled Frank and his companions. Colonel Trevelyan's erect shoulders slumped. For a moment he looked old and beaten. Then with a jerk he faced his grandson. "So be it."

"No!" Lucy Anne darted from the porch to the yard. "It can't be true." Her face convulsed in the flickering light.

"It is true." Frank caught her hands, misery in every line of his body. "Word came, and we rode straight here. That's why my horse is like this. I'd never run him as I did tonight if it hadn't been —"

It's all a nightmare, Silver told herself, chilling in the night air. *I'll close my eyes hard, and when I open them, I'll be in my own bed, dreamin' of my party.* She pressed against the column, shut her eyes and opened them to the same horrible scene.

"Get these horses to the stable," the colonel ordered. His keen eyes swept the guests, lingering on the shivering Silver. "The rest of us will go inside. Ladies, gentlemen, Frank and his friends will change clothing and join us."

A murmur rose as they automatically followed his orders. No separating of men and women tonight. When the colonel suggested the ladies might wish to retire while the men discussed the news, it was gentle Lucy Anne who first protested: "Beggin' your pardon, Colonel, but it will affect us all."

As if he couldn't withstand her pleading, the colonel gruffly ordered, "All right. Gather back in, and we'll wait for Frank."

If she lived to be a hundred, Silver would never forget that time of waiting. Sporadic conversation was pierced now and then by a nervous laugh holding no mirth. Taylor Randolph brought her a cup of fruit punch that she couldn't drink. Lucy Anne's face was ghastly white in contrast to the rosy dress. Only Zach Stuart seemed untouched. He stood a little apart, face somber, saying nothing.

On impulse Silver called him to her. "You don't seem excited."

"I've been expecting it."

She shuddered again and drew the cobwebby shawl someone had thoughtfully provided over her bare shoulders. There was barely time to wonder what he meant before Frank returned, traces of excitement subdued in the great sadness that had invaded his face. *Why, he's a man!* Silver stared in shocked amazement. For one instant she could see why Lucy Anne proudly proclaimed her love. Frank was the replica of his own father.

"Now, Son," there was no censure in the colonel's command. "Tell us everythin' you know."

The fingers that passed over the still-damp dark hair trembled. "Not much more than what I said. Word came to Lynchburg that there was trouble. Anderson's been in charge of the Union forts in the harbor. Rumors have it South Carolina's been ready to attack at Charleston and seize the fort. Anderson's headquarters were in Fort Moultrie, on Sullivan's Island, main entrance to Charleston harbor."

"We know that." The colonel nodded. "Major Anderson moved his troops to Fort Sumter in December, just a few days after South Carolina left the Union."

Frank sent a quick glance at Lucy Anne before he went on, "Fort Moultrie is in Confederate hands now." He swallowed nervously, black eyes strangely dull. "General Beauregard demanded that Anderson surrender. Major Anderson refused. General Beauregard ordered his men to fire." He slumped in a chair as if too weary to go on.

Silver brushed aside her dread and forced herself to spring to her feet. "Why should what they do hurt us? If they want to fight each other, what's it goin' to hurt Virginia? We're a long way from South Carolina."

"We are the South, Miss Trevelyan." Taylor Randolph's nostrils flared. "We'll fight to the death before allowin' northerners to dictate to us."

Silver faced him defiantly. Her instinctive dislike and distrust rose to the surface. Dark eyes flashing, she demanded, "We're just as close to the North as we are to the South! Why can't we just stay in the middle and live the way we want to?"

A jeering laugh answered. "It will never happen." His eyes narrowed even more, sending gleams of blue flame, searing her. "We will have to choose. And the choice will be southern. Any true Virginian will agree."

Stung, Silver's face went deep red then icy pale. "No one can say I am not Virginian through and through, Mr. Randolph." Each word fell like a tiny piece of ice in the silent crowd. "What Virginia chooses will be what I choose."

"Well spoken!" Loud applause rocked the room, sending every tinkling ornament clashing in confusion. The colonel beamed. "A true southern gentlewoman." His colorless face took on a choleric hue. "If the northerners dare to follow up and declare war, we'll fight for homes and families. We'll fight if this valley runs red with the blood of those who came to this grand country in search of freedom. Virginia forever — and not under the rule of tyrants."

A storm of clapping was cut short by the colonel's lifting one hand. "It may not come. Even yet the North may see all we want is to be left alone. But if war comes, we'll go forth in the knowledge God will protect us and give us victory."

Silver ran to his side and slipped one arm through his. "If we have to fight, at least we know God must be a southern gentleman."

This time there was no controlling the frenzied crowd. They went wild, cheering the slender girl with dead-white skin and magnificent eyes, facing them all, a symbol of womanhood.

"Here's to the women of the South!" Taylor lifted high his glass. "We'll fight with chivalry to protect them forever."

Silver's opposition melted before the honest tribute. She had never been so close to liking him. She raised her own glass and drank it to the bottom. Only when she set it down did she notice two glasses had been left untouched. Frank's full glass remained on the small table behind him, partially hidden by a screen of leaves brought in as decoration. Zach Stuart's glass was not hidden. The deep-red punch glowed in its depths, untouched.

"Why, you didn't drink the toast!" she exclaimed without thinking what her words could do.

Dr. Stuart slowly lifted his glass. "I am proud to drink to the women of the South — to all of them." He raised the glass and drained it.

"But you didn't drink to our fighting." Taylor rudely pushed through the crowd until he faced Dr. Stuart.

"No."

How could one word turn the entire ballroom into a mass of speechless onlookers? Silver wondered. Hostile glances made her wish she'd held back her unruly words.

"You won't fight for the South?" Taylor was incredulous.

"I will not." The green eyes were rock hard. "I am a physician. I am called to preserve life, not take it."

"Coward!" Taylor's face blackened with emotion. "Yankee!"

Frank sprang to his friend's defense. "He's no coward, I've seen him fight off three men his size when —"

A rare smile filled the giant's face. "Never mind, Frank, I can defend myself. I appreciate your loyalty." He turned back to the waiting Taylor. "I am no Yankee. I will help sick and hurt and wounded regardless of color or political feelings."

"Then if you aren't a coward or a Yankee, tell me, Mr. Doctor Stuart, just what are you?" The sneer in Taylor's words threw a gauntlet full into the tanned face.

Dr. Stuart raised to full height. For a moment Silver thought he would strike Taylor full in his gloating, ugly face. His eyes turned to steel. Then they fell on Silver, white and waiting. Gradually the anger left his face.

"I asked you a question!" Taylor wouldn't let it lie. "I want an answer, now. *Just what are you?*"

That couldn't be a twinkle in the steady eyes, could it? Silver gasped and held her breath as Dr. Stuart looked into the taunting face opposite and quietly replied, "I am first of all a Christian, then an American, then a Virginian, in that order."

Disappointment threatened to choke Silver. She had unconsciously waited for Zach to defend himself. He had resorted to words only. A faint resentment grew that she had been temporarily swayed by his confession earlier and her own involuntary response to it.

It was the colonel's turn to step into the little circle surrounding the visitor. His face matched Taylor's in color, a murderous red. "You can't mean you won't fight for Virginia?" His blue eyes were colder than Silver had ever seen them. "When every son of Virginia may be needed?"

"I won't be the only one, sir." For a fraction of an instant his eyes turned toward Frank; then he caught himself and went on. "Those of us in the northwestern counties will never agree to leave the Union." His face flamed. "Sir, can't you see what it would mean? Brother against brother. Friend against friend. Look at the state of Kentucky. Ten years ago they demanded gradual freeing of their slaves. That far back they carved a pledge on a block of Kentucky marble, to be placed in the Washington monument, pledging Kentucky would be the last to give up the Union! If war comes, the state will be split wide open. It is already happening. President Lincoln and Jeff Davis, who was inaugurated as provisional president of the Confederate States less than two months ago, were born not much over a hundred miles apart!"

His face gleamed with intensity. "Can't you understand, Colonel? Kentucky will stand true to the Union, but thousands of her sons will join the Confederacy. God help them all when they meet on the battlefield!"

Silver was caught in the whirlpool of his earnestness and stood immovable in front of him.

Not the colonel. Untouched by the guest's oratory, he barked, "What's Kentucky got to do with Virginia?"

"Everything." The simple answer stopped the cry of the crowd pressing closer. Dr. Stuart's defense dropped. Like the colonel, earlier, he suddenly looked old. "If Virginia rebels against the Union, the northwestern counties will rebel against their mother state."

"Never!" Taylor Randolph's arrogant thrust didn't seem to touch Dr. Stuart.

"It's true." Zach's steady gaze to the colonel's face never wavered.

"I've heard such nonsense," the colonel snorted, "but I don't believe it." Yet his hand on the carved cane he carried was not quite steady.

"We have no choice."

"Then you're one of them!" Silver could keep still no longer. Her breast heaved under the delicate lace of her gown. Her heart beat rapidly. All the confusion, anger, and disgust she had felt for Zachary Stuart since their first unfortunate meeting surged to a mighty desire to hurt him as he had hurt her. "You say you are a Christian. Then how can you oppose what is right?"

His face whitened, but he kept his steady look. "Miss Trevelyan, God is neither Yankee nor rebel."

"Then you will fight us?"

"I will never fight — you." The hesitation was imperceptible to all but Silver, whose control was swept away in a flood of color. "I am a Virginian, Dr. Stuart. Any enemy of Virginia will be an enemy of mine."

"And mine." Taylor Randolph stepped forward until his shoulder brushed Silver's. "I hope you someday meet me in battle."

"And you, Miss Trevelyan? Is that what you also hope? To see former neighbors and friends on opposite sides, slaughtering one another in a senseless war to prove who is right and wrong?"

"What will be is not of our makin'." She

51

took her place on the side of the Confederacy in eight words, noting with mingled pain and satisfaction the blow it struck to Dr. Stuart. "Any *true* Virginian would feel the same."

"I see." For a long moment he studied her, until Silver could bear it no longer. In spite of her avowed hatred, something deep inside thrilled to the sadness in his look.

She couldn't face it. She must tear from her mind and heart forever the seed planted, even now growing until she longed to break free from the crowd and be alone to examine it. Frantically she sought for a way to crush the magnetic attraction Dr. Stuart held. Frank had said she couldn't help but love him. Color stained her white face, and she proudly lifted her imperious head, with dark hair dressed in the latest fashion and a few tresses lying on her neck. There was only one way to do it.

Silver turned to Taylor Randolph and smiled brilliantly. Her traitorous heart pounded, but she spoke clearly. "We will discuss war no more. This is my twenty-first birthday, and I have something to tell you all."

For the first time, fear crept into Dr. Stuart's eyes. "Wait, Miss Trevelyan!"

Did the man possess the ability to read

her mind? Silver swept him a haughty glance and opened her mouth, but the colonel forstalled her. With a mighty gesture he thundered, "Sir, you have transgressed every law of hospitality. Go! Now!" He pointed to the open door.

Silver froze. Never in the history of Silver Birches had a guest been ordered away. Regardless of his feelings, Dr. Stuart had come as an invited guest. Even now Frank was coming out of his state of shock and protesting, "Colonel!"

"Silence," the colonel roared. He brandished the carved cane. "Get out of my sight, you — you —" Words failed him.

The initial shock held. Not a sound broke the stillness as Dr. Stuart turned toward the door, shoulders square. Would he go without a word? No. He was turning, looking first at Frank, then at Silver. "If there is ever anything I can do for you, I am at your service." He swung on his heel. Another moment and he would be gone.

The tumult in Silver's heart was replaced by his boldness. In the face of her grandfather's threat, he had dared offer his service, not only to Frank, but to her!

"Dr. Stuart!" Her command brought him about-face.

"Yes?"

Silver ignored her grandfather's protest. "It is highly unlikely we shall require any such service. You see," she dropped her eyelashes then turned to Taylor Randolph with a melting look. "Mr. Randolph and I are to be married, and I am sure he will offer any protection I may need."

She had hoped to wipe the stillness from Dr. Stuart's face. She did nothing of the sort. He merely said, "Good evening, Miss Trevelyan," and half turned to the door.

The split second had given Taylor time to recover. His eyes flamed with triumph, and he snatched her to him and pressed hot lips to hers.

What had she done? What was she doing in the arms of this loathsome creature forcing himself on her in front of everyone? Had she really betrothed herself, promised body and soul to this man? She jerked free and looked toward the arched doorway, almost ready to seek the protection Dr. Stuart had offered.

The doorway was empty.

"Well, well!" The colonel broke the silence. "Silver, you've surprised us all. High time, too! Fill the glasses, Jake," he ordered a nearby house servant. "A toast to my beloved granddaughter and her chosen husband!"

It was done. She was irrevocably bound by her own impulsiveness and desire to hurt Dr. Stuart. Lucy Anne stood by Frank, eyes enormous. Silver turned from the accusation in their depths and the look in her brother's face. "Come," she commanded. "The dance must go on." Taylor captured her, and she led him to the center of the ballroom. "Play," she told the open-mouthed musicians. If she had to face what she had done, it would be with all the control she possessed. Yet the devilish look of passion in Taylor's cruel face frightened her more than anything she had ever known.

Somehow she made it to the end, laughingly putting off Taylor when he would have led her to the gardens. "It's my birthday. I'll stay with the guests." Yet while she won the battle between them, the war lay ahead. She would be trampled by his personality until there was nothing left but ruin. And she had deliberately done it to herself.

Almost she cried out it was a horrible mistake, but the colonel beamed from the corner, and she overheard him telling Lucy Anne, "Just what she needs. She's a mite headstrong. Takes after me, I reckon. Taylor's firm hand will keep her steady."

Silver stumbled, nearly fell. Involuntarily her eyes sought Taylor's narrow blue ones, seeking kindness and respect, seeking love. Only the stamp of success filled those watching eyes, and he pressed her closer until she protested, "Please, Taylor, everyone's watchin'."

At last she escaped. Thank God she was sharing her spacious quarters with no one but Lucy Anne. The minute she burst into the room and locked the door, she flew to the great mirror. Where was the happy girl who had looked back earlier? Who was this stranger facing her from the glass, with tragic eyes and haunted face? And from her throat tore the question that had pounded until it must be engraved on her brain, "O God, what have I done?"

4

When Silver carelessly scratched her name in the rich earth of Silver Birches and laughingly proclaimed the state of Virginia would long remember the date of her twenty-first birthday, she had unknowingly prophesied accurately. Almost overnight the state changed. Abraham Lincoln called for troops to put down the rebellion. It was the match that touched off the building animosity.

"It's done," the colonel announced at dinner one evening.

Something in his voice caught at Silver's heart. She put down her fork on the snowy damask table cover. "What is?"

"Virginia's signed the Ordinance of Secession." There was a strange lack of elation in the colonel's manner. "So have Arkansas, Tennessee, and North Carolina. We're part of the Confederate States of America now." He added heavily, "Taylor Randolph's already gone to offer himself to the military."

"He would."

Only Silver caught Frank's muttered exclamation. The colonel was intent on his subject. Although Silver hadn't confided her feelings about Taylor to Frank, she was sure Lucy Anne had passed on some of the great outburst Silver had been unable to control the night of her birthday celebration. From a thoughtful but often heedless boy, in the past days he had become almost tender in his treatment of Silver.

"No reason you can't be an officer," the colonel announced to Frank. "I've still got connections. I can arrange thin's for you."

Frank's face turned deathly pale, but he said nothing. Only his tortured eyes told Silver how he felt. Suddenly the full impact of war hit her. Her former image of men in uniform gallantly going forth to preserve their way of life, flag of the Confederacy waving against all tyranny, faded. In its place was Frank, the boy who hated killing. Frank, with musket and sword, riding away to kill? No!

The vision haunted her so much she sought him out when the half-eaten meal was over. It hadn't helped for the colonel to add, "Your friend Stuart was right about one thing." Contempt colored his face. "The northwestern counties have pulled out of Virginia! They've decided to form their own state, rule themselves." He added a rough oath, the first ever uttered in Silver's presence. "Those farmers and businessmen don't know what they're invitin'!

They're callin' themselves the Restored Government of Virginia, claimin' they want independence. Rot! All they want's to stay tall with the North."

"Is what they are doin' really any different from what Virginia's just done?" Frank's quiet question lingered in the air behind him as he left the room before the colonel could answer.

Silver found him beneath a budding apple tree, staring across the rolling meadow toward the north. The same misery she'd seen in his face whenever the war was mentioned now shadowed the features so like her own. In some way she seemed to have become younger while he aged. Seeking comfort, she crept close and dropped to the grass beside him, paying no attention to the possibility of ruining the filmy yellow gown she wore.

"Silver?" His eyes sought hers through the growing twilight.

"Yes, Frank." Something in the air choked her.

"I'm not goin' to fight."

Silver was shocked to the core. "You have to! The colonel will make you fight." She shook his arm. "Don't you see? We must stand for what we believe."

"That's why I'll never go." His nostrils

distended. Black eyes flashed into her own. "I don't believe in leavin' the Union."

Every argument Silver had heard her grandfather make rushed to her defense. "Not even to keep the Yankees from runnin' over us? From burnin' our crops and plantations? And just because they're jealous?" Her indignation waxed hotter. "What right do they have comin' in and sayin' how we should live?"

"Is that what you think this war's goin' to be over?"

Silver faltered. "Why — of course! The colonel says —"

"The colonel's wrong, Silver." His quiet words cut through her protest. If he had spoken in anger, she would have matched it. He did not. He spoke as one tired of the whole business. "Have you any idea what slavery really is?"

Silver lifted her head proudly. "I know the slaves on Trevelyan land are cared for better then poor white trash in cities. They're given everythin' they need —"

"Except the right to be free." Frank saw the storm signals in her face. "Besides, Trevelyan slaves aren't the issue. They're only a drop in the bucket. I've been studyin' what it's really about." His face whitened. "If you knew how some of them were treated —" His shudder communicated fear to Silver. "Not so far away, either. The Randolph slaves alone are enough for America to get rid of slavery forever!"

"Taylor Randolph's?" she whispered. "I've heard thin's, but is it that bad?"

"He's a fiend." Great cords stood out in Frank's forehead. "I wouldn't soil my breath tellin' my sister the rotten stuff that goes on. I will say this. I'd rather see you dead than givin' yourself to him!"

Silver was appalled. She had known Frank disliked Taylor, but this! She clutched his arm with both hands. "You must tell me why, Frank. I've given my word. What would the colonel do if I broke it?"

"You don't love him, do you?" Frank's keen eyes pierced the rapidly falling gloom.

"Love him! Dear God in heaven, no! I could never love him!" Silver's tears cascaded in shining trails down her contorted face.

"The only way the colonel would forgive you for backin' out would be if he discovered what Taylor's really like." Frank's eagerness dropped. "No. If he ever did, he'd kill Taylor without hesitatin'."

"The colonel?" Silver couldn't believe it. "Not with his belief in God."

"It wouldn't stop the colonel. At least the slaves on Trevelyan land have never had to fight off their master's attentions, even if they aren't free."

Silver froze. Surely Frank couldn't mean what she thought he did! "Just because I don't like Taylor doesn't mean he's not a gentleman."

"Gentleman!" Frank turned burning eyes on her. "Get it through your head, Silver. No female slave on his plantation is safe when Taylor Randolph's been drinkin'."

"I can't believe you." Silver's breath came in little gasps. "No man could be so low." Suddenly suspicion prompted her. "You aren't just sayin' this because you hate him?"

"Do you think it's easy for me to tell you this?" Frank sounded fierce and buried his face in his hands. "I didn't ever intend to. But I can't see you throwin' yourself away on a beast who's bedded every young female slave on his place."

"Frank!"

"I know. You're shocked and horrified and all that your brother'd talk about what's only discussed in whispers." Frank's bitter words fell on her heart like tiny bullets. "Better you know now than after you've married him." He rose and ran from her as if pursued by a thousand devils.

"Frank, come back." But her call faded in the blackness that had fallen into her heart as well as over Silver Birches. Inwardly bruised, she stumbled to her room, avoiding the family sitting room and the colonel. When Mammy came in answer to Silver's summons, Silver was already in bed. "Tell the colonel I'm not feelin' well, Mammy. I won't be down to prayers."

Would she ever feel clean again, after hearing what Frank had said? For the first time she realized how terrible it had been on her clean-minded brother to bring such stories to her. He would rather have cut off a hand than talk about it. What had driven him to it were love and concern for her.

She struggled to her feet and managed at last to free herself from the cumbersome gown and underclothes that Mammy usually unfastened. The struggle left her wilted, and she was glad to creep back in bed. Thoughts surged through her feverish brain. A scene from long before painted itself in her memory. Her mother had been resting on a chaise longue. Frank toddled around her chair. Happiness filled the room, and when Silver's father stepped in, Silver's mother gave a glad cry. Silver stopped her play to see the look in her mother's face. She never forgot it.

Another scene came, this time of her father. Just a few months before his death, from being thrown while riding, Silver asked, "Daddy, how will I know when I meet the right man?" Her question came from a growing awareness of being fourteen. Friends were already courting and marrying.

"Never marry until he means everythin' on earth to you," Blair Trevelyan told his budding daughter. "Just because your friends marry young doesn't mean you should." His face was half in shadow as he added, "Marry one who will be gentle with you."

Now Silver lay tormented. She could never expect gentleness from Taylor. The vague things she knew about marriage had been gleaned from overheard conversations but were enough to convince her she would never submit to anyone she didn't trust. Yet in a fit of pique she had consented to do just that and with Taylor Randolph.

"No!" She sprang from her bed and paced the floor, her long, white nightdress sweeping a priceless Persian rug. "Not after what Frank told me." Her own declaration of purpose strengthened her. Unable to wait and tell Frank in the morning, she sped to his room. It was empty. The bed hadn't been slept in.

She ran to the top of the great staircase, bare feet giving no warning of her presence. Below her stood the colonel and Frank. Their voices drifted up to her clearly.

"You will either fight honorably for your home and state, or you are no grandson of mine!" The colonel's command was little less than a roar. "If you think I'll have every gossip in the state sayin' I've a coward for a grandson, you're mistaken. I expect you to come to me tomorrow mornin' like a man and ride out with me to make arrangements for you to fight."

Frank mumbled something, but Silver couldn't catch what it was.

"I mean it. You'll go, and you'll fight. There'll be no turnin' back." The colonel shook his fist in Frank's face. "You understand?"

"I understand."

Silver had the impression of armies marching, flags flying, as Frank slowly climbed the stairs. Before he could see her, she darted to his room and waited. The steps slowed and wavered as he came in the door, reeling as if drunk, when she knew he seldom touched even wine.

"Silver!" The low, despairing cry went

straight to her heart.

"Shh." She closed the door behind him, locked it, stood against it as if to keep out hatred and war and bitterness.

"You heard?"

"I couldn't help it. I came to tell you I —" she broke off. There was no time for her troubles in the face of this calamity. "Your bed was empty, and I was alarmed, so I crept to the head of the stairs."

"And heard the colonel practically order me from the house."

"Not that!" In horror Silver's eyes rested on his troubled face. "All we have left is each other and the colonel, Frank. We can't let each other go."

"I know." Frank was suspiciously close to tears. He rubbed one hand across his eyes, the way he had done as a small boy, when he didn't want to cry and show how hurt he actually was.

"You really won't fight?"

"I can't." A fresh wave of misery crossed Frank's face. "Suppose I carry a rifle, get in battle. Even though I've been told to fire, that last moment is my decision. I can't take a life."

"Then what are you goin' to do?" Silver's last hope died in the face of the sunken cheeks and dull eyes facing her. Frank seemed a hundred years old, as if he had skipped manhood and middle age and grown old before her eyes.

"There's only one thing for me to do. Leave tonight."

"Tonight!"

"Yes," he said doggedly. "The colonel expects me to walk down those stairs in the mornin' and say everythin's all right. I can't. I have to get away before then."

"But where will you go?" Silver cried in protest as her world crashed in ruins. She'd never known how precious her brother was to her until then.

"Somewhere away from war and fightin' and hate." A slight shudder shook his slender but sturdy frame.

Like a lightning bolt, audacious words from a stranger came back to Silver. "Dr. Stuart said if there was ever anythin' he could do for us. . . ."

Frank's face caught fire. "That's it! I can go to Harmony."

Silver remembered Zach's strong face. "He can help you. Oh, Frank, take me, too!"

"What?" The word exploded like a cannon. "You?"

Silver regretted her craven cry. She would only slow Frank down. Knowing the colonel, she wouldn't put it past him to follow Frank, drag him back, and force him into service he hated. The girlish lips tightened into those of a woman's. She must not tell him how afraid she was of Taylor Randolph. If all else failed, she would appeal to her grandfather and tell him the truth. She cringed at the thought but smiled at Frank. "You know me. Always lookin' for adventure."

It seemed to satisfy Frank. He turned toward his room, scanning the luxurious appointments, at last seizing a light bag nearby. "I won't be able to take much. Just what I can carry."

"Let me call Luke."

"No! That darky would tell everythin' he knew." Frank's fingers were already selecting and rejecting garments, discarding fancy ones in favor of sturdy clothing.

"Then I'll get dressed and drive you to Lexington, where you can get a coach."

"I can't go that way, Silver." His voice stopped her as she fumbled with the locked door. "Grandfather would trace me."

So he knew as well as she how the colonel would react. "How will you go?"

"On foot."

"Impossible!" Silver stared as if he had taken leave of his senses.

Frank's mouth set in a straight line as he led her to a small desk. "No, look." He pulled a piece of paper from the drawer and began to draw, talking as he worked. In seconds he had sketched a rough map. "Here's where we are." He X'd the spot. "Here's Harmony." He made another X almost due north. "It's about a hundred and twenty-five miles, near as I can figure. Once I'm past Lexington, I'll hit the woods."

Only one thing registered with Silver. "A hundred and twenty-five miles! How will you ever make it? You don't even know if there are trails!"

"I have no choice."

Silver was silenced.

"It won't be so bad." He managed a crooked grin that didn't reach his eyes.

"If the colonel follows. . . ." Silver swallowed hard. The room swam. "He can use the hounds."

The Trevelyan pride raised Frank's head. "I'm smarter than any hound. Besides, Dr. Stuart told me how escapin' slaves outwit pursuers. They wade in streams and branches for miles at a time. I'll have a night's start, Silver. Maybe more. If you'll slip out early and let King Blair out, maybe the colonel will think I've gone for an early ride."

"Take King Blair," Silver pleaded. "At least as far as Lexington. You can leave word there you're goin' on to Richmond."

Hope flared, settled to dull, gray ashes. "I won't lie, Silver. I don't want you to lie, either. Just say you aren't sure when I left or where I was goin'. It won't really be a lie. You won't know exactly when I leave." The suffering in his face was more than Silver could stand, and she turned away. "I couldn't bear having you wavin' good-bye when I leave. It's hard enough knowin' I can never come back." His voice broke in a sob. This time he made no effort to hide his tears.

Silver threw herself into his strong arms. "When the war's over — and everyone says it won't take long to lick the Yankees — you can come back!"

"I can never come back," he whispered into her hair. "The colonel will never forgive me. Tell Lucy Anne not to hate me. Someday maybe I can send for her — if she'll come."

Silver raised tear-wet eyes. "She will. She loves you."

"Can you slip down to the kitchens and pack some food?" Frank shattered the fragile moment.

"No, but Mammy can," Silver said.

"She'll be lurkin' 'round my room to see if I really am sick."

"Can we trust her?"

"With our lives." Silver cautiously unlocked the door and stepped into the now-silent hall, grateful the colonel's room was at the far end.

"Mammy," she beckoned the faithful slave outside Silver's door. Putting a finger on her lips, she led Mammy into Frank's room. "He is goin' away. The colonel wants him to kill, and he can't."

Mammy's oxlike eyes gleamed, but she said nothing, only wrinkled her face in deep sympathy.

"Get me food for several days, Mammy. Enough for a week, at least. Anythin' I can carry, dried stuff. Put it in a knapsack and bring it here." Frank smiled at her, and Mammy disappeared out the door.

It seemed like hours before she returned, panting a bit from her secretive trip to the kitchens. "Heah yo' is."

"Thanks, Mammy. When the colonel asks, don't tell him anythin' except I said I was ridin' into Lexington in the mornin'."

"I doan' no nothin', Massa Frank." She rolled her eyes. "God be a-blessin' yo'." She crept out the door and back to Silver's room. Frank slipped into the other part of

71

his rooms and came back wearing rough clothing.

"I don't want to remember you cryin'," he told Silver gruffly. "Someday, we'll be together again. Don't worry about me. I'll be all right. Burn the map. It mustn't be found! Even if the colonel has suspicions, he won't be able to prove anythin'. I won't stay at Harmony. I'll go wherever Zach thinks best." A poignant light filled his eyes. "I wanted you to like Zach. I never did get to ask how you liked your red and green and tan present."

Silver longed to hold him close, confess the arrival of the "present," and laugh over her indignation that now seemed childish. There was no time. He must go. Every minute counted.

A final embrace and he was gone, leaving an empty, sore spot in her heart. He had finally agreed to ride King Blair to Lexington, but disappear from there. Instead of turning the magnificent animal over to anyone, he would simply free the horse he loved. King Blair would come home.

The night hours melted into dawn, and Silver lay sleepless. She could visualize Frank riding to the edge of Trevelyan land, turning back with twisted face, or perhaps not looking back. He had been right. He was severing any tie with Silver Birches that had ever existed. The colonel would never forgive. Frank's legacy would be that of knowing he was despised by his grandfather.

In spirit Silver rode every step of the way with Frank. Finally she saw him reluctantly dismiss King Blair, burying his face in the horse's smooth mane, letting his arms clutch the satiny neck for the last time. She saw him slap the horse's rump and order, "Home, Blair!" then turn his face to follow the North Star.

As dawn broke so did Silver's heart. Zach Stuart had been right again. Already, the war that had begun the night of her birthday was tearing families apart because of loyalties that seemed impossible to reconcile.

"Good-bye, Frank," she whispered to the world brightening outside while her own heart was dark — and mentally she pictured him stepping into a stream to hide all trace of where he had trod.

5

In spite of her worry, Silver's weary body demanded sleep. She woke hours later to sunlight streaming through the open drapes. A feeling of foreboding possessed her. Something hard and crumpled dug into one cheek. She impatiently drew it out. It was the crude map Frank had drawn then ordered her to burn.

Halfway to the fireplace she paused. The crumpled piece of paper brought back the terrible love and relinquishment of her brother's face. She carefully smoothed out the creases and hid the tiny paper in her desk. The next instant she retrieved it. Someone might clean and find it.

She would either have to destroy it or keep it with her at all times. Unaccustomed fingers finally stitched a small case from an old handkerchief corner and fitted it inside her bodice. It gave a comforting spot of warmth to her chilled heart.

The colonel's roar floated upstairs as she stepped into the hall. "Jake, where's that grandson of mine?"

Silver's heart stopped then caught again as the rich Negro voice said, "I doan no, Massa."

"Silver!" There was no denying the anger in the call.

With an inarticulate prayer for help, Silver ran lightly down the stairs, catching up her morning gown of pale pink and pausing at the foot of the stairs. An errant ray of sunlight targeted her, from the open front door, and some of the colonel's crustiness vanished at sight of his favorite.

"Have you seen Frank?"

"Why, he said somethin' last night about ridin' to Lexington today." *Please, God, don't let him ask when Frank said it,* she prayed silently.

"I ordered him to come down and go with me to offer his services as needed to the Confederacy." His eyes bored into her. "Do you know anythin' about how he feels?"

Silver's heart leaped. Could she make him understand? "He's never wanted to kill, Colonel. You know that."

"Squeamish."

"No." She shook her shining dark head. "He just loves all creatures. Can you even begin to imagine Frank killin' a man?"

"He'll have to." The colonel struck his boots with his riding crop. Evidently he'd already been up and out surveying Silver Birches. Other plantation owners might leave full control in their overseers' hands.

Not the colonel. He personally checked conditions every day of his life.

A wave of pity for the troubled old man before her filled Silver and gentled her voice. He really was old. She had just never seen it before, since he was robust and strong. "Colonel, Frank will do as he believes right, but it will never change his feelin's about you and Silver Birches."

She thought her plea had scored, but the colonel threw off any sentimentality in favor of what was. "He'll do as I say, or he's no kin of mine!"

"You don't mean that." Silver stepped closer and peered anxiously into his face.

"I do! The boy's got to become a man. If Virginia fights — and God help us, she's goin' to have to — then Frank will fight along with her." He stamped into the dining room and threw his crop on an upholstered chair. "Bring us our breakfast, Jasmine."

The young slave in the neat housedress swept him a frightened glance. "Yassir."

After she scurried out, the colonel courteously seated Silver then himself. "Child, I don't like this business any better than you or Frank. I'd give anythin' I own to prevent war. Now that it's comin' fast, all we can do is play our parts. The states have a right to rule themselves. God was with those early settlers who carved homes out of wilderness. Virginia, virgin land, and free. Your grandmother and I left Pennsylvania, came out here years ago, built up Silver Birches. We fought every step of the way. Indians. Poverty. Sickness and storms."

He waved through the many-paned window to the stretching land that was his. "It's my life. No one can tell me how to run it."

"But isn't our leavin' the Union kind of like — like —" She groped for words. "Suppose an arm says it won't be part of the body anymore. Isn't it still part?" Lucy Anne's question, now asked of the colonel.

"We've a right to be let alone." The colonel threw back his head the same way Sultan did just before he stamped and snorted. "They say it's because of slavery. That's only a side issue."

Silver noticed the veiled look in Jasmine's eyes as she deftly served the usual huge breakfast. Yet even the fresh-cured ham, light biscuits, and honey seemed stale today. How would it feel to be in a room where someone talked about you as if you were a piece of furniture, without feelings or hearing? It was a new thought. Slaves were slaves, weren't they? Yet it had power to make Silver wait until the girl left the room before speaking.

"Colonel, is it true some plantation owners —" the words *Taylor Randolph* hung on her lips. "I — Someone said slaves are —" she couldn't finish. A burning blush rose from the lacy collar of her gown.

"There are always owners who abuse their slaves. They will answer to God for it." The colonel liberally added honey to a biscuit dripping with freshly churned butter.

"I mean the women —"

"We do not discuss such thin's in this house." The colonel impaled her with a single glance. "The wickedness of men will be held to their account." He dropped the biscuit and glared at her. "If Negroes had never been brought from their homes across the seas, it might have been better for everyone. But they were brought. They're here, and they've got to be handled. A man has the right to rule his property." He leaned forward in his earnestness, "I heard the other day there was some kind of count taken. There are roughly 400,000 slave owners in the South right now. There are roughly four million slaves. That's ten to one. Can you imagine what'd happen if four million slaves were set free?"

His fist crashed to the table, setting the silver jumping. "Where'd they go? Who'd take care of them? They're better off where they are."

Silver picked at her food. Never before had she given thought to much more than new clothes, such household duties as were required of her, and running free on Sultan.

The colonel wasn't through. "Granted, there are men who mistreat their slaves, same as men mistreat fine horses. The wise ones are those who take care of them, see they're fed and housed and clothed. Why," he boasted, "there's not a slave on Silver Birches that isn't better off than any northern Negro walkin' the streets of the cities!"

Silver caught the scornful glance of Jasmine as she poured more coffee. The colonel was wrong. His slaves weren't as contented as he believed, if the bland face with the telltale eyes gave any indication.

Silver slowly left the table, more confused than ever. The colonel's parting words followed her, "God created male and female, bond and free. All have their place. That's the way it is." He had crashed his fist against the table again. "And by all that's holy, that's the way it's goin' to stay, so long as I live and can do anythin' about it!"

It was so different from Frank's story the night before! Who was right? *Why did all this have to come up and spoil everything,* she thought petulantly. Life had been so good before! She aimlessly wandered to the large porch running around the mansion, hating the war inside herself. It was probably all Zach Stuart's fault. He would feel about slavery the way Frank did and had passed it on, she'd just bet.

Unwilling to be alone with her thoughts, she ran back inside. "Colonel, I think maybe I'll ride over to Lucy Anne's."

"Fine." He accompanied her back outside and ordered a groom to fetch her horse. "Frank should be back soon, and we'll get on with it."

"You really don't want to force him, do you?"

The colonel's face darkened at her impulsive words. "I have no choice." He strode off toward the stables.

Strange, that was what Frank had said, too. If only the war would come and go, so they could all go back to their own lives! Yet even as Silver wished, she knew it was impossible. There could be no going back.

She fled upstairs and burst into her room. Mammy was directing an upstairs maid in cleaning her room. Thank God she'd put that paper in her dress! "Mammy, I want to talk to you. Alone."

Something in her voice straightened the big woman from her kneeling position. She turned to the girl. "Go 'long wif yo'."

Already Silver was regretting her whim, but there was no turning back with the wise, dark eyes fixed on her. "Mammy, are you happy?"

"Happy!" The big eyes rolled. "Wif my chile to keer for? Why yo' ask me that?"

"All this talk of slaves and bein' free, I guess." Silver forgot her intention to ride to Lucy Anne's. "I just wondered — what's it like, bein' a slave?"

Silver had never seen the look in Mammy's face that came, then went so quickly she wondered if it had been real. A look of pain, mingled with regret, quickly covered. "Mighty fine on Tr'vl'n land."

Even though she felt as if she had opened a door without knocking, Silver persisted. "You came here just before I was born, didn't you, Mammy? Where were you before?"

Her innocent question shattered Mammy's control. Slow, heavy tears spilled down the dark face. It was the first time Silver had ever seen Mammy cry.

"I'm sorry, Mammy." She flew to the woman and leaned her head on the capacious lap that had comforted her so often. "I just realized I never asked about you before. Why . . ." She drew back. "You've always been here. The other slaves have families. Why don't you, Mammy?"

"They wus tuk."

"Took? Who took them?"

"Massa Wilson. He own big plantation. Big debt cum. Massa Wilson sell Mammy." She lifted her snowy apron to hide her working face. "Sell pickaninnies. Three. Sell man. Never see no mo'."

Silver was aghast. Selling slaves was nothing new to her, but she'd never been touched by its tragedy. "You mean he *separated* you, Mammy?" Her voice shrilled in the bright room gone gloomy. "In all the years you've been with us, you've never known where they were?"

"Gone."

Sudden suspicion filled Silver's questioning mind. "Did the colonel know all this when he bought you?" She bit her lip and tasted the sickish sweet blood. "He didn't buy you and leave your family behind, did he?"

"No, chile. Massa buy me when man, pickaninnies done be gone."

Such a few words to cover the tragedy of a life! A few days before, Silver might have felt sympathy and dismissed it as her shallow life swept on. Not now. Her parting with Frank was too close.

"Mammy, at least you have a home with us." She turned away to hide the sight of the whimpering woman who had served faithfully, with never a word of her secret sorrow. Determination filled her, and she quietly descended the stairs and sought out the colonel. "Why didn't I ever know about Mammy?"

Bushy eyebrows lifted. "Why should you? It was a sad affair, but there was no changin' it."

Rebellion stirred, and she set her chin, so like her grandfather's. "You mean she 'has her place' and should be content."

As if on the defense from her quiet attack, the colonel protested, "I tried to trace her husband and children. I'd have bought them. They were gone long before I got Mammy. The plantation owner shot himself soon after, knowin' he was ruined. The heirs had no records of who bought the field hands and children." He scowled. "Mammy should be flogged for disturbin' you."

Silver steadied herself with an effort. "Maybe I should be flogged for never even carin' enough to ask." She flounced away.

"Don't you go gettin' involved in thin's

that are no concern of yours," the colonel warned.

Silver spun on one heel, but before she could reply, pounding hooves caught the colonel's attention.

"I suppose that's our young scalawag comin' back from Lexington." Relief warred with anger in his face.

Silver's heart threatened to choke her from where it seemed to have lodged in her throat. The next minutes would be terrible.

"It's King Blair, all right. I'd know his cadence anywhere. After all I said, Frank's runnin' him again." The colonel marched toward the sound of the coming horse. "What's this? The saddle's empty!"

King Blair easily swung into the pasture leading to the stables. He hadn't run far enough to be winded.

"The boy must have been thrown and hurt!" The colonel stared at the horse. "Get my horse, Sam!" An openmouthed Negro ran to obey. "Silver, get water and bandages ready."

She couldn't let him go this way. Silver stepped in front of her grandfather. "He hasn't been thrown."

Her stilted words stopped the forward march of the colonel. "How do you know?"

"Because he —"

Again she was cut off by flying hooves. This time Lucy Anne Simmons and Calico pelted into the yard. "I heard King Blair racin' past our place! Where's Frank?"

"He's gone."

"You mean *dead?*" Lucy Anne swayed in the saddle.

"No!" Silver forced the words through her constricted throat. She closed her eyes against the stormy anger in the colonel's face and the white misery in Lucy Anne's. "He couldn't bear to kill. He left sometime last night, said he was goin' to Lexington. I'm not sure when he left or anythin', except this war has already come to Silver Birches."

Lucy Anne slid to the ground and shook Silver. "He can't have gone without one word to me." Her despairing cry mingled with the colonel's, "We'll bring him back. We'll search every road from here to Richmond, but we'll bring him back." He shook his fist at Silver. "When we do, he will fight like a man!"

Silver could bear no more. "He *is* a man, Colonel, can't you see that? You've taught him to do what he knew was right. You should be proud he is doin' it, even if it is dead wrong in your eyes!"

The colonel breathed heavily. "And in

your eyes? Will you turn traitor to Virginia, as Frank has?"

"He has not turned traitor," she denied passionately. "He loves Virginia! But he cannot do for her what is against everythin' he believes in."

"He will, when we catch him."

"Let him go!" Lucy Anne ran to the colonel and clung to his arm. Her wide brown eyes held fear.

"You say that? When he's denied you as well as his home?"

"You can drag him back. You can send him to fight. But he won't." Even Lucy Anne's lips were chalky. "He'll go to battle and be shot down before he will ever raise a gun and kill." The quiet certainty shook even the colonel. "If you bring Frank back and force him into the army, Colonel Trevelyan, you will be just as guilty of his death as if you signed the order of execution and led him in front of the firin' squad."

She was magnificent. Her earlier fear had evaporated. "Will you send him to his death, simply because he is carryin' out the very standard of bein' true to himself you taught him?"

Silver reeled. Had anyone ever dared speak to the colonel the way Lucy Anne had just done? Her love for Frank had transcended natural shyness; she was like a mother bear fighting for her cubs.

The colonel took a shaken breath. For one terrible moment Silver thought he would throw Lucy Anne aside and rush after Frank. Then he said, "So be it. From this day, I have no grandson." He turned his back and stalked toward the house, shoulders erect.

Lucy Anne sagged. She had won, but it was a hollow, meaningless victory. "Silver, I —"

"Come to my room. I'll tell you everythin'." Silver's heart wrung with pity for her friend. Again she felt younger, less able to cope, than the girl beside her.

"What started it?" Lucy Anne asked, bracing herself against the padded back of the couch in Silver's suite.

"I was troubled last night and went to find Frank." She hesitated. Not even to Lucy Anne could she repeat the things Frank had told her about Taylor Randolph. She went on to describe finding the empty bed and hearing the conversation between her grandfather and Frank. "When he came back in his room, he looked as if he'd already been mortally wounded. He said he couldn't fight. He was goin' away."

"To Dr. Stuart's."

"You *knew?*"

"The minute I saw King Blair comin' home."

"I didn't want you to know. I was afraid your father'd make you tell the colonel."

"Frank never came right out and said it, but it was there. When you love someone, you can feel what's inside," she finished softly.

"He said to tell you that someday he'd send for you, if you'd come." Silver was glad to be able to add the final message from Frank.

"I'd go anywhere on earth Frank asked me to."

"You really love him that much! To give up home and family and Virginia?"

Lucy Anne's soft eyes smiled at Silver's incredulous question. "I do. It's the only way any woman should love a man she marries." She sighed and pressed her hands together in their soft riding gloves. "Someday you'll meet someone and know what I mean. Someone strong, and gentle; someone who will have been waitin' for just you all his life."

Why should Dr. Stuart's face, dappled with shadows as it had been on the porch that night, intrude into their conversation? His voice, clear as crystal, filled her mind: "May I come back to call . . . with your full knowledge of why I will come?"

Resolutely she shoved it away, yet even when Lucy had taken a reluctant farewell and disappeared over the rolling hills separating their homes, memory of Lucy Anne's confident prediction haunted Silver until she could barely stand her own company.

6

Zach Stuart leaned his head wearily against the inside of the jolting coach and closed his eyes. He was so tired even his eyebrows drooped, but it was not physical fatigue. Many times he'd gone without sleep in the course of his duties. Why should a simple ride from Silver Birches to Lexington leave him exhausted?

He remembered the shame in Frank's face as he led the way to the stable and ordered a mount saddled. "To think you should be ordered away!"

"It's all right," he had assured the boy, compassion sweeping aside his own problems. "War will do more than separate people." He swung easily to the saddle, heedless of his dress suit. "God bless, Frank." A hard grip of the other's hand and Zach turned his horse north, leaving the white-faced friend to face whatever came, wishing desperately he could somehow stop the fires of madness that would lead to destruction.

He didn't remember much about the night ride. He was vaguely aware of his horse's easy gait and surefootedness even at night, but his thoughts were far away. His trip to Richmond had begun in anticipation, and the medical convention where he met and chatted with some of the leading doctors in Virginia, as well as heard lectures and observed new techniques, more than fulfilled his hopes. He was going home better equipped for his profession.

At Lynchburg he had run into Frank Trevelyan, and the warm liking they'd had all those months before, when he cared for the boy, sprang into renewed friendship.

"You must stop at Silver Birches." Frank's face glowed. "The colonel and Silver would never forgive me if I let you get this close without stoppin'."

Zach had protested. He needed to get back.

It had been useless. "A day or two won't make that much difference. You said yourself everyone was fine when you left Harmony."

Zach had to admit the truth of Frank's statement.

"Besides, it's my little sister's birthday," Frank wheedled, dark eyes filled with mischief. "I promised her a special treat. You're stayin' here for a few days. Then when you get ready, come on out to Silver Birches. I should get there before you do, but if I don't finish my business, just introduce yourself and tell them I sent you."

"I'll have to get your sister a present. Do you think a doll would be nice? I don't know much about little girls."

"A doll will be fine."

Why should Frank's grin make Zach uncomfortable? Was this Silver a tomboy or a spoiled child or something equally unpleasant? Nevertheless, he purchased the finest doll he could find in Lynchburg. He packed it carefully, along with his good suit. Even a little girl's birthday party might be an occasion for dress clothes. Southern plantations were known for extravagant dress.

Zach's first sight of Silver Birches had been overwhelming. Accustomed to more sturdy farm homes, he had thought Richmond the epitome of elegance. Now here in this gentle valley lay a mansion. He guided his horse along the curving road beaten smooth by countless hooves, eyes fixed on the gracious home ahead. It sat against a background of verdant green, its whiteness as bright as if it had been freshly painted the night before. Great columns rose to support the stories, with verandahs sporting ivy and flowers. The trees for which the house was named lined the way and shimmered in the air. Only threat of storm tore Zach from his contemplation of the house. He climbed down from his horse, stiff from his ride, and pulled the bell rope beside the front door.

"Yassuh?" A beaming black face split with white teeth greeted him.

"I'm Zach Stuart, a friend of Frank's. Is he here yet?"

"We'se expectin' him." The friendly servant led Zach upstairs. "Make yo'self to home."

When he had gone, Zach looked around the room he'd been given and laughed. He'd have no trouble making himself at home. Luxury quietly shouted from every corner of the room, yet tastefulness had been used in the rich furniture and velvety rugs. He freshed up from his ride and threw himself on an inviting couch, a wry smile crossing his rugged features. Wait until he told the folks about this little side trip! A snatch of Scripture from the well-worn family Bible danced through his brain, ". . . many mansions." Well, he might one day have a heavenly mansion. Right now he'd just enjoy visiting an earthly one.

The drum of rain and distant hoofbeats awakened him. The room had grown gray with shadows. Zach sprang up, rapidly changed clothing, and brushed his fiery hair. He was ravenous. What time was supper served? Or would it be dinner here?

The trace of a smile lingered on his good-natured mouth as he stepped into the hall. Voices came from belowstairs, and he headed that way, his loping stride eating up the long hall. Frank must have arrived! Good. Armed with the doll, so he could get Frank's approval, he rounded the corner.

Crash!

Appalled, Zach looked down. A drenched young lady sprawled at his feet. In spite of her wetness, she was the loveliest thing he'd ever seen. A chord quivered in his heart, which had been strangely silent, as he helped her up and murmured something about how clumsy he was, aware of another girl's smothered giggles.

She couldn't really be hurt, could she? She wasn't answering.

Suddenly it seemed imperative to make her understand. He haltingly explained his presence and showed her the beautiful doll.

The girl was no longer silent but raging. He slowly became aware of what had happened, but not before she and her friend disappeared down the hall.

"So that's Frank Trevelyan's little sister!" His overdeveloped sense of humor exploded in a laugh. Now what? He'd better make amends. He trod the hall to the partly open door, his steps making no sound on the Persian runner. He was just in time to hear the girl Silver say, "Not if he were the last man on earth. I could never, never, love a creature like that!"

Something primitive rose within him, the fighting spirit of the Scots. "*Never* is a long time, Miss Trevelyan."

A long time — a long time — the wheels of the coach repeated his words and brought Zach back to the present. He was glad he had the coach to himself, except for a huddled figure, opposite, evidently asleep. So much had happened in such a short period of time! He had never believed in falling in love at first sight, yet he had succumbed to madness over Silver Trevelyan. Everything within him rose to accuse him. She was unfit for the life of a doctor's wife. She was shallow and vain and a rebel. She believed God was a southern gentleman!

He stifled a roar of laughter mingled with bitterness. Yet he could not stifle his memories of her: the way she looked that night at dinner, no longer soaked, but gloriously imperious as she neatly turned down Taylor Randolph's bid for his own. Her white shoulders and arms above the soft dress with rosebuds. Didn't she know better than

95

to kindle fires such as burned in Taylor's eyes by wearing such apparel? Women could be fools sometimes. How would Silver look in a soft gray dress such as his own mother wore? Or kneeling by a hearth, with a child clinging to her soft-blue skirts?

Vexed at his visions, he forced himself to relive that one day he'd had with her. When he'd asked her to save dances, there had been a look in her eyes that belied her coquetry, a look of pure innocence and hidden depths.

The combination of moonlight and Silver clad in her blue ball gown had proved too much. In the shadowy porch he had stated his intentions, asked to be permitted to call. His face burned hot at the memory. Cool, unstampedable Zach Stuart, practically proposing to a strange girl the day after he met her? Impossible!

What would she have said if Frank hadn't burst in?

Zach licked dry lips. She might have laughed him to scorn for daring intrude on such short acquaintance. Yet, what if she — he clamped down the lid of the emotion bubbling inside him.

In rapid-fire succession the events of the evening swept over him. He had made an enemy in Taylor Randolph, if not Silver herself. As for the colonel! Zach could feel again the scorching anger that had driven him from Silver Birches.

A low moan from the other occupant of the coach jerked Zach back to the present.

"Are you all right?" His sharp eyes and keen perception drove everything away except that single sound of suffering.

There was no reply, and the crumpled figure curled into a smaller ball, as if to turn all attention from itself, but another moan came and was stifled in a worn sleeve.

It was enough for Dr. Stuart. His firm brown hand gently uncovered the frightened face — and froze against the edge of the blanket.

The face was a rich, chocolaty brown — and the eyes were terrified.

The meaning of what he saw drove home to Zach instantly. Somehow a runaway slave had managed to get in the coach, with or without the driver's knowledge. Yet the suffering eclipsed all other considerations.

"Where are you hurt?"

The boy, little more than a child, pointed to his right leg.

Doctor though he was, Zach cringed. The angry mass of infection surrounding deep cuts spoke of one thing — chains. The putrefying odor that had been masked by blankets threatened to overpower him. He leaned far out and breathed in a great draught of fresh air. His movement attracted the driver's attention. "How is he?"

Gratefully Zach said, "Pull over, will you?" The driver had known. Was this why there were no other passengers and why when Zach appeared the driver had been startled and muttered something about this bein' no regular stage?

The coach lurched into a nearby stand of trees, far enough from the road to be seen only by passing birds. "Whoa!" The driver nimbly hopped down and came back to the coach door.

"Help me get him out." Zach was already lifting his medical bag.

It took a half hour to cleanse and bind the wounds to Zach's satisfaction, while the driver watched the road. "I guess folks is so excited 'bout the war news they ain't payin' no attention to other folks," was the driver's comment.

"Who is he?"

The driver shook his head. "Doan know. He was in the coach when I harnessed the team this mornin'."

Zach's eyes bored into the driver's face. "You know the penalty for helping runaways?"

He would never forget the driver's

answer. "I know what Jesus'd do."

The firm grip of hands said the rest. Zach's heart leaped. Here was a common, even poor driver, if the looks of him could be believed. Yet he was helping someone, though it meant endangering himself.

"Where are you taking him?"

Eyelids like hoods dropped over the driver's eyes. "I got a place." He swept the doctor a knowing glance. "Least you know 'bout it, the better off you'll be." He swung to the seat. "Ready?" He didn't wait for an answer but shouted, "Giddap!" and the coach began its swaying journey again.

Understanding crept into Zach's being. So this was why the road between Lexington and Harmony was so rough! It wasn't the well-traveled one he knew, but some back road the driver knew well. Zach had been too busy with memories of Silver Birches to notice, when they pulled away.

Late that evening the driver pulled up before a tiny farm, nearly hidden by the hollows and hills, where it nestled in a grove of trees. "Wait here." He was gone a few minutes and returned with a tall man whose face was dim in the sputtering glow of a turned-down lantern. Zach asked no questions but gave low instructions on how to care for the wounds, then climbed back in the coach. In an incredibly short time he felt the coach settle to a more comfortable pace and knew they'd gone back to the main road. He dozed, Silver's scornful face as she proclaimed her engagement to Taylor Randolph floating above him.

"Hold up there!" A harsh voice roused him to blackness of night, shot through with one piercing gleam.

"Whadda ya want?" Could that really be the surly voice of the driver who'd been so helpful?

"We'll just have us a look inside."

"Help yourself. Nobody there but a sawbones headed home."

Zach closed his eyes as the light came nearer, then opened them as a rough voice bellowed, "Who're you?"

"Dr. Zachary Stuart, heading toward Harmony."

"Where you been?"

"Medical convention at Richmond." Good thing he'd changed out of that dress suit before starting the coach ride.

"Reckon you're all right." The light swept the coach interior.

Zach forced himself not to glance at the corner where the wounded man had curled. "Are you looking for someone?"

"Runaway slave." Even the tone of the

man's voice was ominous. "When I git him. . . ."

"No runaway here." Too late Zach realized relief had colored his voice.

The lead rider peered into the coach, eyes gleaming. "What's that?" He pointed to a dark stain on the seat, touched it and smelled it. "Smells like blood. Fresh blood."

Zach's skin literally crawled. Only his professional manner and training to hide emotion allowed him to laugh carelessly. "Scratched my hand on a thorn bush when we stopped to drink from a stream." Thank God it was true! He held out one finely shaped hand, marred by a long ugly red scratch still oozing a few drops of blood.

A rough curse shattered the stillness. "Good thing fer you it's red enough blood." Eyes gleamed like a wild animal's eyes. The rider backed out of the coach and away.

"Good work, Doc." The whisper came out of the darkness after the band of men were gone; then the coach started on.

Zach drew a ragged breath. So this was how it felt to be hounded, followed, and chased down. Every bone in his body rose in protest. Why couldn't the colonel and Silver see the great wickedness slavery could bring? Yet to be fair, there was no sign of mistreatment of slaves at Silver Birches.

Word got around, and even in Harmony the Trevelyans were known as God-fearing, conscientious plantation owners.

Not so Taylor Randolph. Zach's lip curled. The whole state of Virginia knew what kind of man he was — except the colonel and Silver, evidently. Surely she had only been venting her anger by announcing that she intended to marry the cur! Something inside her would keep her from going through with it. He groaned, much as the runaway had done earlier. Spiritual anguish was only lifted as he bowed his head and in a few unspoken sentences put the girl he had met and learned to care for in her Heavenly Father's care.

Zach was glad to reach Harmony. He bade the driver farewell and pressed an extra bit of money on him. The man's red-rimmed eyes filled with poignancy. "Someday, we'll meet again, God willin'." His Adam's apple slid up and down. Zach waved him out of sight, thinking how even a shabby, dusty coach could be a chariot of mercy and a tired driver, an angel in disguise.

It was good to be home! To be back working with those who needed him, away from the charm of a girl who had sworn herself his undying enemy. Yet after the most demanding days, her beauty haunted him. Days turned to weeks, and gradually she became a lovely memory. He had accepted she was not for him. He drove himself even harder, working relentlessly in fighting battles against sickness, poverty, and ignorance.

Then one day when he wearily dragged home to the simple farmhouse that was home, his mother met him at the door, an excited look on her usually peaceful face, fingers over her lips. "Shhh! He needs all the rest he can get."

"Who?" Zach flung down his bag and crossed to the prone figure occupying the couch by the fireplace. He could scarcely keep back his exclamation. Sound asleep, tousled black hair dark against a snowy pillow, lay Frank Trevelyan. His face was thin. Dark circles underlined his eyes. One hand was flung out in total exhaustion, scratched, dirty fingernails and all.

Zach listened to the boy's heartbeat, decided his mother was right, and followed her back to the porch, closing the door behind him. "When did he come?"

"About an hour ago. He stumbled up the road, gasped out his name, and said he'd been told he was headed the right way." Her voice was filled with concern. "I tried to get him to eat something or to get him to bed. He said he was too dirty, but if he could just rest." Tears sparkled like diamonds on her lashes, giving her the appearance of a white-haired angel. "He tried to tell me why he was here, but I wouldn't let him. I told him to wait until you came."

"Good for you!" His steady eyes met hers. "You probably already realize he may be hauled back to Silver Birches."

She only nodded, and Zach marveled, as he often did, at the strength within her. "We can only wait and see."

It was two days before Zach would allow Frank to tell his story. When he did, he asked Mr. and Mrs. Stuart to also be there. "You may as well know," he told them, a trace of mist softening the beautiful dark eyes that reminded Zach of Silver. "I'm an outcast. Disinherited. Disclaimed. I've lost everythin', home, family . . ." He couldn't finish the sentence.

"Not your sister's love. Nor Lucy Anne's." There was no standing on ceremony in moments like this. Zach strode across the living room and looked down at Frank. "I can't believe either of those girls will ever turn you away."

A spark of some of the joy that had been Frank's touched his face for an instant. "I don't know about Lucy Anne. But Silver still loves me." He seemed to cling to the thought. "I can even see somethin' good from all this. If I hadn't been leavin', I don't know if I'd have had the nerve to tell her what a rotter Randolph is." He dropped into brooding silence. "Silver confessed she'd never loved him. She was caught up by all the talk about North and South. After she learned the truth about Taylor," he kept his gaze steady, even though color stained his still too-pale face, "she despised him. She will tell the colonel the truth before she'll ever marry Taylor Randolph."

Zach couldn't keep his heart from singing. "Good for her!" He saw the puzzled glances between his parents at his fervent exclamation and added, "I've been praying something would happen to keep her safe."

"Prayin'!" Frank sat bolt upright. "For Silver?"

"Of course." Zach smiled at the boy so recently turned man. "For you, too."

"I need it. I can't go back. I won't fight." His head drooped. "Best thing for me's to get out of here before the colonel comes chargin' up here after me."

"You're safer here than anywhere else," Zach reminded. "I doubt if the colonel will suspect you've gone here any more than some other place. He'll naturally check Lynchburg, even Richmond, first." He asked sharply, "Was there any sign you were followed?"

"No. At first I thought every rustle was someone after me. But after the first few days I realized it was just the wood's sounds." He shivered. "It was still kind of scary."

"Nothing to be ashamed of, Son." Mr. Stuart smiled at him. "Many's the time I've been startled on a dark night."

"Bide with us a while," Mrs. Stuart encouraged.

"I could cause trouble. If they come for me, I'll run."

"At least stay with us until you get rested. Time enough for worrying over what's round the bend when you have to take the road."

"Thank you, Mrs. Stuart." Frank turned away. Zach was sure it was to hide his feelings. "I'll stay, at least for a few days." He managed a grin. "I may even surprise you. I'm not bad with chores." He stuffed a cookie from the plate on the nearby table in his mouth and said through it, as if to hide his feelings again, "Can we send word I'm all right?"

"When the time is right." Zach leaned against the mantel, struck again at the strong resemblance between Frank and Silver. "I'll be listening around town and know when it's safe." He turned to his father. "Isn't it time for worship?"

During the Scripture reading and prayer, Zach quietly observed Frank. He seemed open, more free of bitterness than when he first came. What if Frank stayed here with them and learned more of God? The greatest gift the Stuarts could give him would be freedom — not from the colonel, but the freedom of knowing his Heavenly Father loved and cared for him.

The thought of Silver crept unbidden into Zach's thoughts. He had successfully banished her to the far recesses of his heart. Then Frank came — and with him, every gesture and look of the mistress of Silver Birches.

Zach's heart raced. This time it was he who turned away so his feelings could not be seen by the others. Even if he never saw Silver again, he could be thankful to God for delivering her from her own impulsive actions. The war that might ravish Silver Birches was nothing compared to the total destruction of mind and spirit Silver would experience as Taylor Randolph's wife. And if or when the fighting was over and peace began its healing work, a day might come when a visitor from Harmony would again be welcomed by a girl turned woman, who had shaken his hand and promised to be his friend, before the world went mad.

7

Uneasy weeks hung over Silver Birches. Gone were the balls, hunts, and gracious living Silver had always known. In their place was the specter of war. Rumor piled on rumor, leaving a grim and unseen shadow across the plantation. Frank's name was never mentioned. An unidentified courier had delivered a single-word message to Lucy sometime after Frank's disappearance. The one word, *peace,* had been scrawled on a much-creased, dirty scrap of paper. Lucy Anne and Silver figured it must be from Frank. He could not send the word *harmony* without endangering his position.

Corroding bitterness against the world itself had begun its deadly work in Silver's life. How could the God she'd believed in since childhood forsake the South or even let families be split? "Seems as if God would smite our enemies and get it over with," she complained to Lucy Anne one bright June morning when they had ridden to their favorite spot on the promontory overlooking the lush valley. Field hands were busy. Stillness lay over the scene, yet it was not a peaceful stillness. Silver had seen the same look in other slaves' faces as the one that had crept to Jasmine's at breakfast morning the day Frank turned up missing.

"God led the children of Israel out and drowned their pursuers. Why doesn't He hurry up and get it done, so we can get back to normal living?"

"We'll never go back to where we were." Lucy Anne seemed thinner, more frail than she'd been when they last sat on the spot. The shadow in her eyes didn't quite leave even when she laughed. "Besides, God was leadin' His children *out* of captivity, not preservin' a way of life that *is* captivity."

"You sound like an abolitionist!" Silver sat bolt upright, eyes flashing.

"I've been watchin' a lot of things since Frank left." She idly plucked a tiny flower and stroked its velvety soft petals.

"So what?"

Lucy Anne threw down the flower. "I've been findin' out the slaves aren't so happy as their singin'."

A tremor ran through Silver. "They're fed and clothed and cared for when they're sick." She sounded like an echo of her grandfather.

"They're also beaten and sold away from their families." Lucy Anne's even tone never faltered. "And sometimes the women

110

are — mistreated." Scarlet rose in her tanned cheeks, but her eyes met Silver's.

"Did Frank tell you . . . ?"

Lucy Anne was horrified. "Of course not! No gentleman ever speaks of such things to a lady. I've overheard my father decryin' the practice. He says it's against all that's holy." Lucy Anne's brooding eyes turned from Silver to look into the valley. "Still there are a lot of awfully light children in the slave quarters." She bit her lip, and Silver saw a bright stain appear. "Especially at Taylor Randolph's plantation."

It was out in the open between them. Silver didn't know whether to be glad or sorry. "So you know!"

"How could anyone help it? He isn't even careful about talk." Indignation roused her. "I'm surprised the colonel hasn't horse-whipped him for even darin' to call on you!"

"Maybe he doesn't know. Frank —" She steadied her voice. "Frank said the colonel would kill Taylor, if he knew what was goin' on."

Pity swept across Lucy Anne's anger. "You aren't still goin' to marry him, are you?" She shuddered. "I couldn't. To know he was that kind of fiend and marry him would kill me."

"Of course I'm not goin' to marry him,"

Silver snapped. "I was a fool for ever announcin' I would, but I —"

"You were tryin' to get back at Dr. Stuart for standin' up for what he believed after he'd paid attentions and sparked your interest."

"Are you a mind reader?" Silver's face took on the same hue Lucy Anne's had held moments earlier.

"Frank said you were bound to love your present." Some of Lucy Anne's usual mischief sparkled in her brown eyes.

"I don't love him. I hate him. I wanted to show him I didn't care a pin about him."

"So you claimed Taylor and have regretted it ever since. When are you tellin' him you won't marry him?"

A dark shade dropped over Silver's eyes. "I don't know. I've made it a practice to avoid bein' alone with him." Shivers of fear splintered along her spine. "I'm scared to death of him, and I've never been afraid of anythin' in my life. Maybe it's because of what — what we've just been talkin' about." Revulsion filled her. "At least he's been busy soldierin' and hasn't been over too much. Maybe he'll get into battle and be killed. He deserves it."

"Not him." Lucy Anne's lips curled in contempt, and she picked another flower. "He'll be the kind to get a commission and stay safe behind the lines, plannin' how to send his men into battle. You'll not get out of it that easy."

Lucy Anne's words recurred as Silver swept downstairs to dinner that night. Her light-green gown picked up the freshness of June and framed her shoulders and arms with froth. Even though they weren't giving parties, the colonel expected her to dress for dinner as usual.

Voices stopped her on the threshold of the dining room. "I say she's dawdled long enough. I want to marry her before I go." Taylor Randolph's drawling voice had an unusual crispness to it.

"You'll get no argument from me." The colonel laughed. "Might be a different story from her. Oh, Silver," he caught sight of her in the doorway. "Come in. Taylor's been pushin' for an early weddin', and I see no reason we can't go ahead." His mouth was pinched. "Since I no longer have a grandson, it'd be handy to have Taylor."

Every bit of blood seemed to drain from her heart, leaving her frozen. Her quiet voice startled her. "I don't aim to marry a man who's off to get himself killed."

Devils danced in Taylor's cold eyes. "Are you refusin' me?"

If only she could scream out that was just what she was doing! She didn't dare. She should have told the colonel long ago how she felt. Now she had to compromise.

"You all say the war's goin' to be over in a few months. A weddin' can wait." She coolly seated herself as Taylor drew out the high-backed chair. Her fingers trembled, and she hid them under the folds of the snowy tablecloth, shredding a lacy handkerchief to relieve her feelings.

Taylor's mouth set in a stubborn line. "I want to marry you before I go. I demand the weddin' take place this week."

Coquetry shone in the eyes that would have liked to scorch him. "I told you, Taylor, a bride wants her husband with her, not gone." She almost choked, even though what she had said was true enough.

He gave in with bad grace. "Oh, all right. Have it your own way. I'll have my way soon enough once we're married." His suggestive leer was lost on the colonel but succeeded in bringing an angry blush to Silver's face and neck. She lowered her eyelids to hide her fear and hatred.

After he rode away, arrogance in every line of his body, stiff with anger because Silver had turned her face away from his demanding farewell kiss, Silver scrubbed her lips and cheeks hard with the remains of her handkerchief.

"A strange way to treat a fiancé's caresses," the colonel said dryly from the foot of the great staircase.

Distraught by her inner fight about Taylor, Silver didn't check her words. "I will never, never marry him as long as I live!"

"What?" the colonel's face purpled. "You gave your word. You will live up to that word. No granddaughter of mine will shame me the way. . . ."

Silver knew he was referring to Frank. It should have warned her how raw the open wound still was. It didn't. She was too filled with her own misery to be understanding. "Do you think I'll marry a man who has bedded every female slave on his plantation?"

Shock and something unexplainable filled the colonel's face. The next instant he raised his hand, struck her full across the lips. "You wicked creature! Who's been fillin' you with such lies?"

"They aren't lies." The only blow her grandfather had ever given her had roused depths of anger she hadn't known until now existed. "Are you blind and deaf? What about all the light-skinned pickaninnies on his place?"

"Hussy!" There was a suggestion of foam on the colonel's lips. He raised his cane as if to strike her down, then dropped it. "Taylor Randolph came to me like the man he is. He had heard the rotten gossip. He traced down the facts. It isn't Taylor who is responsible. It's his overseer Jenkins. When Taylor found out what was happening, he flogged Jenkins within an inch of his life and ran him off the plantation. And you — you dare to stand there condemning this patriot, neighbor. . . ." He couldn't go on.

"You actually believe all that?" Their faces were similar as she faced him, even while all hope for his understanding and protection seeped away. "Everyone in the county except you knows the truth."

"I'll hear no more of this. How dare you question your grandfather?" Never had she seen him so livid. "I say Taylor Randolph is a fine Virginian and a southern gentleman. You will marry him, if it's the last thing I do on this earth!"

Silver wanted to shriek, to demand that he take it back. She did neither. She silently turned and marched upstairs, the wraith of memory accompanying her. So had Frank walked, after his final discussion with the colonel. Apprehension touched her. Would the day come when she would also have to

116

flee, to save her honor, as Frank had done? It was a sobering thought. Automatically her fingers felt for the tiny bag with the little map. If all else failed, if Taylor Randolph came through battle unscathed, she would try to get to Dr. Stuart. He could send her on wherever Frank had gone. Comforted, she smoothed the bag back in place.

Tension mounted even more as a few days later the colonel stormed into the house. "Said I was too old, they did." He grunted his disgust. "I tried to enlist. If one Trevelyan won't serve, another should. They sent me home and said I was more use here."

In spite of her hurt over Taylor, Silver was touched. "They're right about you bein' needed here." She quickly glossed over the age question. "I don't know what's got into our slaves, but if you're gone even for a day now, thin's don't seem to get done the way you want." Her brows drew together. "All this talk of bein' free is ruinin' discipline."

The problem increased. A smashing southern victory at a small stream called Bull Run, south of Washington, D.C., put an end to the North's plan of marching on Richmond and ending the war in ninety days. United by rejoicing and trouble among their slaves, Silver and the colonel shelved personal differences. The colonel carved the date of Bull Run, July 21, 1861, in the post outside the corral gate, to commemorate Virginia's blow for freedom.

There was no question about any wedding now. Taylor Randolph and others from the valley were engaged in the business of war. Silver often felt she'd been given a reprieve. The colonel was too busy singing praises of "Stonewall" Jackson to give much attention to her problems.

Another problem had claimed Silver's attention as well. There was something terribly wrong at the Simmons home. Lucy Anne didn't know what it was but said it was somehow connected with the visit of a foreigner to the valley. "He's from one of the Deep South states," she reported. "My father almost seems afraid of him! I don't know why he lets him stay when he comes. I'd send him packin'." She spent more and more time at Silver's as the stranger continued to call. "He looks like he's borin' clean through me with those pig eyes. I don't like bein' there, and Daddy said it's fine for me to stay here with you."

Summer droned on. Reports of the name Taylor Randolph was making for himself drifted back, along with news of the northwestern counties. They had provided for the formation of a new state to be called Kanawha and already were sending troops to the Union armies for training. Bull Run had shown the sad lack of skill in fighting. About 18,000 poorly trained volunteers had made up each side. Obviously both sides needed more than the will to win, although the South had gained great prestige, both at home and overseas.

One sultry night in mid-August Lucy Anne and Silver lanquidly fanned themselves on a screened verandah. Their talk was as lazy as the soft night. In the north, a streak of lightning flared the sky, giving promise of needed rain. The colonel was away on one of his endless errands, seeking a slave who had disappeared from the fields that morning.

"Have you had slaves leave?" Silver asked.

"One or two." Lucy Anne's wilted rosebud shone white against her rich brown hair.

"I wonder why they want to escape, when they've always been treated good."

"Freedom's in the very air, I guess. They're all stirred up over the war and speeches they pass on from one to another."

A rustling of leaves and Zeke, a house slave from the Simmons plantation, stepped to the house. In the moonlight his dark face was ghastly. "Miss Lucy, oh, Miss Lucy. . . . It's terr'ble."

"Am I needed at home?" Lucy Anne had been spending a week with Silver.

"No!" The Negro's eyes rolled. "Doan yo' go home." Sheer terror shone in his face as he tossed a paper in her lap and backed away. "Massa, he say, 'Tell Miss Lucy go — quick.' " Zeke disappeared into a night suddenly grown alien.

"Whatever —" Lucy Anne clutched the paper.

"Quick, we'll go to my room." Silver's sense of perception caught something evil in the very air they breathed. "Mammy," she ordered the big woman who came at her call. "Miss Lucy Anne and I are not to be disturbed. Understand?" She didn't wait for an answer but dragged an unprotesting Lucy Anne up the stairs.

"I'm afraid to read it," the younger girl sobbed. "Here, Silver, you read it." She thrust the paper out with shaking hands.

"It's a letter from your father." Silver glanced at the signature.

"Then he must be all right."

Silver didn't answer but read silently. Every trace of color fled from her skin, leaving it pure as alabaster. It couldn't be true! No, it was too incredible. She dropped the paper, looked at her friend.

"What is it, Silver?" Lucy Anne clutched Silver's arm. "Is my father all right?"

It took every ounce of courage she possessed for Silver to gasp, "Lucy Anne, your father is dead."

"Why, he can't be!" Lucy Anne cried. "He was in good health when I left. Dead? Impossible." Yet she backed away from Silver, eyes kindled with fear. "Give me the letter, Silver."

"Not now." Silver tore herself free of the shock still gripping her. "Lucy Anne, you've got to get away from here. Tonight. Now."

"But why?"

Words trembled on Silver's lips and were bitten back with superhuman effort. She grasped Lucy Anne's cold hands in her own. "Will you trust me? Can you believe you must get away from this valley, even from Virginia, now?"

Lucy Anne sagged in her clutch. "How can you ask such a thing?" A new fear shot into her face. "Is it that stranger? Reynolds?"

Silver couldn't keep back the hatred in her eyes. Lucy Anne had her answer.

"It *is* Reynolds. Has he murdered my father?"

"No! But your own life is in danger." Silver compressed her lips tightly.

"Silver, in God's name, what is in that letter?"

Silver's tongue moistened her parched lips. Could she bring herself to tell Lucy Anne the truth? Slowly she formed the words; they wouldn't come.

She tried again, discarding the idea of telling Lucy Anne the whole truth. "That man Reynolds, he knew something about your father. And — and about you. Your father left word before he died that you were to go as quickly as you could, anywhere where Reynolds can't get to you. You're only seventeen. Your father's gone. You've no one to protect you against Reynolds."

It didn't seem possible a face could turn any whiter, but Lucy Anne's did. "I never even heard of the man before he came. How could he know about me?"

Silver hesitated. Would Lucy Anne fall to pieces if she were told the truth? She didn't dare chance it. "We're leavin' tonight. We're goin' to follow the map Frank left and get to the new state, where you'll be safe." Her strong will overpowered Lucy Anne's objections. "I've never asked much of you, but I am now. Once we get away from here, I'll tell you everythin'. Can you trust me until then?"

"You mean you're leavin' Silver Birches, takin' me away somewhere?"

"I have no choice." The words burned into Silver's brain. "Besides, it'd be just like Taylor Randolph to show up wantin' a weddin'. The colonel won't protect me. Don't you see, Lucy Anne, we have to go. Both of us."

For one moment childhood bonds between them strained, then held. "I don't know why, Silver." Lucy Anne bowed her head. "But I'll go."

8

The lazy evening had suddenly become a nightmare. Silver felt as if she were reliving the night Frank left. Only this time there was no Mammy to help. "We can't even let Mammy know," she told Lucy Anne. "The colonel would be sure to find out she was coverin' up somethin' —" she shivered. "After tonight, I don't know what he'll do." Memory of that single blow heightened her fear.

In spite of their hurrying, it was past midnight before the two girls were ready. Silver had stolen to the kitchen and snatched all the easy-to-carry food she could stuff in a sack. She had gone into Frank's room and removed two sets of his old clothing, struck by the chill of the room that once housed her teasing brother.

"You mean we have to wear those?" Lucy Anne was aghast at sight of boy's clothing. "Trousers?"

"Yes." Silver shut her lips in a hard line. "We'll travel as two boys fishin'. We're small enough, so no one should notice anythin' strange." But when they started to put caps on, it was useless. Their long, thick hair wouldn't cram under the caps.

Silver reached for a pair of sharp dress-making scissors on her dresser.

"What are you doin'?" Lucy Anne muffled a scream.

"It's the only way." Closing her eyes then determinedly opening them and facing herself in the mirror, Silver slashed into her beautiful dark hair.

"You said you'd never cut it, except to save your life."

"That's just what I'm doin'." Great locks of curls fell to the floor, surrounding her stoutly booted feet. When she was free, she shook her head to hide the tears welling up. "See?" The cap went on easily.

"Why, you look just like a boy!"

"So will you." Silver ruthlessly cropped Lucy Anne's hair to her pink ears. Perhaps the grimness and haircutting did what even explanation could not do. Lucy Anne sat submissive, as if actually grasping for the first time what lay ahead — and behind, if they did not get away.

"At least it's summer," Silver whispered as the clock struck one ponderous gong, and she opened her door. "I'm glad it's startin' to rain. It will wash out tracks." She put one finger over her lips and motioned Lucy Anne to follow. Down the long hall, past the colonel's room, carefully avoiding stair treads that squeaked, they slipped out the door. "We're safe so far." Her mind raced. "They won't follow until at least mornin'."

"Who?" Lucy Anne demanded, but Silver shook her head. With a scared glance both ways, Lucy Anne ran after her, across the open yard to the shelter of a great maple.

"Where are we goin'?"

Silver was struck by the dread in her voice and the little hand that clung for protection. "To your place."

"But Zeke said no!"

"It's the only way. When Reynolds and whoever he gets to help him find out in the mornin' that your father's dead, they'll rush for Silver Birches. First they'll beat out of Zeke that you got a message, so they may be expectin' you to try to escape. The last place they'd ever think you'd be would be home." With lightning rapidness her brain worked, planning. "We'll take Sultan and Calico as far as your home then send them back. The colonel will remember Frank did that same thin' from Lexington, and that's where they'll head."

"The servants will see us," Lucy Anne objected.

"We aren't goin' to the house." They had reached the stables, and Silver slid the door

126

open. "We're goin' to that old abandoned icehouse the far side of your place." She carefully led out Sultan, then Calico. "We'll ride bareback." Through the darkness she peered doubtfully at Lucy Anne. "Can you?"

"I have to, don't I?"

Admiration beyond anything she'd ever known filled Silver. It also settled her own churning stomach. Lucy Anne would bear what still was to come, even the truth. Silver clenched her teeth at the pain the thought started and softly told Sultan, "Shh!" Every nerve in her body ached from tension. What if Sultan or Calico neighed and brought someone?

The rain not only had come, but was drumming steadily as the two girls mounted. "Lucky we brought heavy coats." Silver settled aboard Sultan's broad back, thrilled at the freedom of wearing pants and riding astride instead of the usual side-saddle. "Ready?"

She felt rather than saw Lucy Anne nod.

The storm broke with fury, as if protesting their wild ride. Flashes of lightning followed by thunder crashing as if hurling boulders into a canyon mingled with the rain. An exultant spirit caused Silver to laugh aloud. Her cry would be drowned in the storm. "They'll never trace us, Lucy Anne."

The plodding figure was drenched but valiant. In a flash of lightning, liquid brown eyes shone through the storm. Never had Silver loved her more.

Even though she's — Silver smashed the wicked voice inside. "We're almost there."

They dismounted in front of the dark shape of the icehouse. With a final pat, Silver started Sultan home.

"What if Calico won't follow?"

Lucy Anne's terrified question froze Silver's blood. "She will." She gave Calico's rump a hard smack. The mare, unused to anything but Lucy Anne's gentle touch, backed away then galloped after Sultan, leaving the girls alone.

"Ugh! It's all spiderwebby." Silver brushed the hanging threads from the half-rotted doorway and stepped inside. The next instant she struck a match and stared in amazement. "What on earth —" The icehouse that should have been filthy was strangely filled with unexpected smells, not the musty, mouldering smell she had expected, but the human smell of unwashed bodies.

Silver whirled to face Lucy Anne's enormous eyes before the match went out. "Is anyone usin' this?"

"N-no." Her fingers bit into Silver's arm.

Sudden suspicion filled Silver. "Someone has been!" She struck another match, but there were no clues as to why that smell was there.

"Frank said once that escapin' slaves used places like this to hide." Lucy Anne swallowed. "Do-do you suppose this could be one?"

"It might." Silver carefully snuffed out her match and felt her way to another crumbling door. She pushed it open. Its hinges groaned in protest. Almost she expected to have someone leap at her, but they couldn't stay here not knowing if danger lay beyond that door. Cautiously she struck a third match — and gasped. Before her was a rickety table with a kerosene lamp. She instinctively put her hand on it. Instead of the coldness that should have been there, the blackened chimney was still warm, although as if it had been blown out perhaps an hour or so before.

"Whoever was here is gone." She pulled Lucy Anne inside, then relighted the lamp, turning the wick low so the glow only faintly lit the cavelike room. "We're safe here."

"What if they come back?" Lucy Anne's eyes were nearly black in their intensity.

"Since it's stormin', they probably won't.

Besides, we don't have anywhere else to go yet." She pointed to a dim opening. "If we hear someone comin', we can sneak out there." She stepped to the narrow aperture and peered out. "We can squeeze through. It must lead to the river."

"At least there's a blanket." Lucy Anne trembled. "Silver, now that we're away from Silver Birches, why are we runnin'? Am I — Was I right? Am I insane?"

"Of course not!" Silver turned from the anguished face.

"Then why is everythin' so strange? Daddy dead, us here, you sayin' our lives were in danger?"

It had to be done. Silver couldn't avoid it any longer. Yet how could she tell Lucy Anne the terrible secret her parents had kept so long? She moistened her lips, forced the words through her constricted throat.

"Lucy Anne, you're part Negro."

For a full minute Lucy Anne didn't move. Hadn't she understood? Silver watched her age before her eyes, as she had once seen Frank do. Would she burst into hysterics?

"Read the letter." The words came from Lucy Anne's very soul.

In the dim light of an abandoned icehouse Silver took the crumpled letter from her shirt, where it had lain next to the map.

130

Ironic, freedom and bondage so close. She forced her low voice to steadiness.

Dearest daughter,
I would give all hopes of earth or heaven to keep from writing this letter. There is nothing I can do to stop the terrible Fate that lies ahead. By the time you receive this, I'll be dead. It's the only way.

Silver ignored the low moan of pain and forced her chattering teeth to be still, hating her task as she'd never hated any task before.

Years ago I was a guest on the Florida plantation of a man named Reynolds. I met a girl. She looked enough like you look now to be your twin. She had the freedom of the plantation, and at first I took her to be a guest. The greatest shock of my life was learning she was a house slave, a glorified slave with certain privileges. She was a quadroon, born of mixed-blood parents. Her grandmother had been a full African Negro: her grandfather was white — and a cousin of Reynolds.
I was mad for her. By the time I learned

her race, it didn't make enough difference to even halt my desire. I tried to buy her. Reynolds laughed in my face. He had other plans for her. They turned my blood cold. She would become just one more in a string of conquests to him.

I waylaid her on every opportunity. I knew she was growing to care for me, and one night when everyone else was out hunting coons, I persuaded her to run away with me. We weren't even questioned. No one looking at her could suspect she was other than white.

We stopped and were married by an official too sleepy to ask questions, especially when I paid him a great sum, mentioning "family pressures" as the reason for our awakening him so late. I knew the law would never recognize our marriage, but at least in the sight of God I had tried to do what I could.

I thought of taking her far away, but thought of my plantation here held me. Florida was a long way off. Perhaps Reynolds wouldn't even connect my disappearance with hers. I left a note I had been called to Washington on business, and as soon as I brought your mother here, I hurried to Washington and sent a wire.

Years passed. During those years you were born. I don't think anyone ever loved a child the way we loved you. The devotion of your mother, pure and encompassing all her life, had changed my early passionate desire for her into a steady glow that brightened our lives. Yet always the shadow of fear hung over us, the fear of discovery. Legally she was not my wife or your mother, but a slave of Reynolds.

The Compromise of 1850 renewed our fear. Fugitive slave laws allowed slaveholders the right to claim slaves by merely presenting proof of ownership before a magistrate. Heavy penalties were imposed on anyone interfering with recovery of a runaway slave or helping him escape.

You used to wonder why your mother cried so much. She lived in the shadow of discovery. Yet she was so honest, so convinced of a need to do what was right, she made me promise that before I ever gave my consent to your marriage, I must tell you the truth. I promised. Still I have dreaded the day, wondering if you could ever understand, or forgive. . . .

I've watched you and young Frank Trevelyan, and trembled. If he's like the colonel, he won't be able to accept your race. Yet I've seen signs he loves you not only with love of your beauty, but your soul. If you get away from here safely and find Frank, you'll be able to tell the minute he hears the whole story. If there is doubt in his heart, it will show in his eyes.

You can guess the rest of the story. Reynolds came. He saw you, innocent, the picture of your mother. The same passion that inflamed him twenty years ago rose. I never told you our home was mortgaged to the hilt. Somehow Reynolds got control of those mortgages. Everything is his. I cannot afford to pay.

He demanded you. He would never give you even the self-respect of an illegal marriage. My price was to be his silence. I could never agree but told him I had to have time. Today he made his final demands. Either I agree or he will bring in the authorities and seize you, as well as all my possessions. I told him he would have his answer in the morning. I didn't think he would consent, but he did — only after telling me that if I refused, he would take you, and when he was through with you, sell you on the auction block as a common field hand!

He maintains that as the child of a runaway slave, an illegitimate in the sight of the law, you are subject to his rule, especially as there is blood relationship between you.

Lucy Anne, I could never get you away safely. I am stalling him the only way I know how. One bullet, and my life will end. Perhaps in the confusion, it will give you a little more time to run, hide, anywhere! Don't tell anyone the truth except Silver. She loves you. Even though she will be horrified at this, I can't help feeling she'll help you. Remember, don't let her risk too much. She will be in danger as well as you, if it's found she helped you escape.

God forgive me for what I have done to you, beloved child, daughter of your mother. Maybe someday when you marry and have a child of your own, you'll understand and even have pity on

Your loving father

Silver was openly weeping when she finished. The lamp sputtered and went out. Its final ray mercilessly targeted Lucy Anne. Despair lined her face.

Silver sprang across the narrow space separating the two shaky chairs. "Don't look so! Your father was right. I love you. So does Frank. Do you think this will make any difference to him?"

"I don't know." The lifeless voice struck Silver to the heart.

"It won't. Why should it?"

"Can you honestly tell me there's no difference with you, Silver?" Lucy Anne asked. "Why, I don't even feel like myself. How can it help makin' a difference? Don't answer. Not now. Tomorrow mornin', no, today, you can go back to Silver Birches."

"Never!" Silver clung to the younger girl. Words to reassure her rushed to her throat and were cut off. Everything she had been taught about Negroes, their "places," the inferiority, warred against love for the girl who had taken the place of the sister she'd never had. One thing she could honestly say: "I will never forsake you. It isn't any safer for me at Silver Birches than it would be for you. All the dangers aren't from people like Reynolds." In bitter tones she told how the colonel had struck her and finished with, "I never thought I'd tell another livin' soul that. But you have to understand I'm as afraid as you are."

"What if we do get to Harmony? They can still come after me there."

"Not if Dr. Stuart can get you through to Canada on the Underground Railroad. It's said the escape route goes through Pennsylvania. The colonel was shriekin' about why more weren't caught and sayin' what he'd do if he ever found anyone helpin' his slaves when they should be grateful for what they had at Silver Birches." She added, "I love him, but your father was right. You can expect no help from him. Neither can I."

For hours the girls huddled together, silent yet unified. A common cause, trouble for both, had welded an already strong love. Once Silver dozed, but roused to feel a single tear slipping down her hand. "What is it, Lucy Anne?"

"If I look in Frank's eyes and see anythin' but love, I'll wish I'd stayed here and died."

Her words haunted Silver. When the girl drifted into an uneasy sleep, Silver still sat staring into the darkness. How would Frank feel, knowing Lucy Anne was part Negro? Child of an illegitimate marriage? Daughter of a slave? What if he turned away in disgust?

"He won't," Silver whispered to the gradually lightening room. "She's white." Yet the law said that anyone even one-eighth African was a Negro.

"Lucy Anne's different," Silver assured herself, knowing she lied. There was no difference between her and others whose skin was darker. Was this why Frank had been adamant about slavery? Had he heard of or met those with stories as tragic as their friend's?

Silver allowed herself to speculate what would have happened if they hadn't left. Vivid pictures rose in her imagination: a terrified Lucy Anne backing away from Reynolds; Lucy Anne trembling on the slave auction block. In Silver's nightmarish scenes Reynolds took on the appearance of Taylor Randolph as his tiger-fierce eyes possessed her. They almost became one in her thinking. She had seen a slave auction once while on a trip with the colonel. It had been days and weeks before she forgot the look in the young girl's eyes as she stood before gloating bidders who called out rude words that Silver didn't understand and of which she could only guess the meaning. The colonel had quickly taken her past.

How could she have forgotten? This was part of slavery, too, Frank had reminded her. It still hadn't touched her. Not until it threatened to reach out and destroy Lucy Anne. There had been signs. Jasmine's contempt. Her own feeling of wondering how it felt to be treated as a piece of furniture. Mammy's story.

Mammy would be getting up about now.

Although the steady rain effectively hid the hour, the plantations would be stirring. Early rising was the rule, except for Silver. What a contrast between this place and her room. Would she wake in her own beautiful bed and grope for blankets to chase away the cold nightmare? No. This was reality. That bed, Silver Birches, the colonel, even Sultan, were gone forever. She could no more go back than Frank could. She, too, was an outcast. Even worse, she was a criminal the law had every right to arrest and punish for helping a runaway Negro.

"But Lucy Anne's not a runaway slave!" she protested violently, then caught her breath as Lucy Anne stirred. The bit of light from the large crack in the wall showed dark rings under the sleeping girl's eyes. She must rest to face whatever was ahead.

Could it be possible any court would give her to a man like Reynolds? Yet the courts only carried out the law. Doubt assailed her, left her weak. In the eyes of the God the colonel worshiped, was that law valid? A second thought left her shaken: Could it be possible God was not a southern gentleman after all — but a Yankee? Yankees were against laws that would send Lucy Anne into worse than slavery.

Too tired and confused to sort it out,

Silver allowed her head to droop, the boy's cap fell from her short-cropped curls, and from sheer exhaustion she slept.

9

Drained by emotion and lack of rest, the two girls slept in each other's arms. The hue and cry raised on the Simmons' plantation when it was discovered the master had shot himself didn't carry across the fields to the old ice-house. Neither did the contorted features of Reynolds trouble them as he learned he had been cheated again. Muttering words that even gentle Lucy Anne would have known were indecent, he mounted and spurred his horse cruelly, arriving at Silver Birches at mid-morning.

"Where is she?" He burst into the dining room unannounced. Only Jasmine was there to answer, and she merely stared. "Where is she, I say?" He wrenched her arm and brought a cry of pain.

"What's the meanin' of this?" the colonel boomed from the doorway, riding crop held high. "Just who are you, sir, to come into my house and treat this girl so?"

The authority in his voice halted Reynolds. He dropped Jasmine's arm, and the girl fled sobbing. "Beggin' your pardon, colonel, but I've come for what's rightfully mine."

"Nothin' on my plantation belongs to

such as you," the colonel roared. "Get out!" The cane waved menacingly.

"Lucy Anne Simmons is mine," he muttered a blasphemous phrase. "Her mother was one quarter Negro and a slave of mine, as well as a distant cousin." His eyes were black with evil. His sensual lips curved in a cruel smile. "She's here, I understand?"

The colonel didn't flinch. "What proof have you got?"

Reynolds triumphantly pulled out papers, validated by officials.

The colonel reeled from the blow. The next moment his military training brought him straight. "Why come here? Take it up with her father."

The dining room rang with Reynolds's maddened curses. "He's cheated me! I own everythin' at his place." Forgetting the cane, he hissed, "Includin' his daughter. When I'm finished with her, she goes on the auction block." He ended with another string of curses.

"Stop!" The cane descended with all the anger the colonel possessed, square across the shoulders of the sneering intruder. "No matter what you claim, no man talks like that in my home. Now get out! When you bring a sheriff to prove what you say's right, I'll talk to you. Go!" He raised the cane again. "I'll see you in hell before I'll turn Lucy Anne or any girl over to you."

"Then I'll drag her out," Reynolds threatened. "You'll pay for this." Rage twisted his ugly face into that of a gargoyle. "Reynolds doesn't forget. You're aidin' and abettin' a slave, and —"

"Get out!"

Reynolds fled, much as Jasmine had done.

The colonel, breathing heavily, blindly groped his way to a chair. His blood boiled. That trash, coming into his home, demanding Lucy Anne. It must all be a monstrous lie. Yet when Zeke came panting in a little later, crying, "The massa done shot hisself!" Colonel Trevelyan was beside himself.

"Mammy, call Miss Silver," he ordered the frightened woman who appeared at his jerks of the bell rope.

"Why, she ain't here, Colonel."

"Not here!" He riveted her to the door with a glance. "Where is she?"

"I doan no. She lef' a note." Mammy produced it from her capacious white apron pocket.

The colonel snatched it, read it aloud.

"Dear Grandfather —" Strange, she never called him anything but "the Colonel."

143

Foreboding filled him, and he tried again.

Dear Grandfather,

What I told you about Taylor is true. I can't marry him. There's no use arguing, so I'm going away. Don't try to find me. I'm twenty-one and responsible for myself. But Grandfather, remember — I love you and Silver Birches. If this horrible war ever ends, maybe you can forgive me, but I will never marry a man like Taylor Randolph. Not even if it means giving up Silver Birches and you forever.

Silver.

The colonel's eyes burned. "When did you find this? When did you last see her?"

"Why, last night with Miss Lucy Anne." Mammy's big eyes popped. "Somethin' the mattah, suh?"

"She's gone. What did she say?"

Mammy shook her head disbelievingly. "She jus' say she an' Mis Lucy Anne wuzn't to be disturbed."

"What time was it?"

Mammy turned her gaze full on the trembling Zeke. "Jes' after he come."

The colonel wheeled. "You were here last night?"

"Yessuh. Massa Simmons tell me to give letter to Miss Lucy Anne." His thick lips closed. He did not repeat the final message, "Go, quick," he had also delivered.

"Did you know last night that Mr. Simmons shot himself?"

"No, sah." Zeke was on safe ground now. "Massa Simmons done tol' us darkies we 'served a ev'nin' off. We-all had a big singin' an' shoutin'. No one heerd no gun go off."

The colonel was halfway up the stairs before Zeke finished. Striding down the hall, he jerked open the door to Silver's room. Everything was in order. There was no sign of a hasty flight. "What's missin', Mammy?" he asked the heaving woman who'd followed him.

She ran through the closet. "I doan rightly no. Miss Silver's done got so much."

By the time Reynolds got back with the sheriff, the mystery was still unsolved. Silver had been wise enough to gather every lock of hair, every trace to show hasty flight.

"This is the man who refused to give up my slave," Reynolds pointed a shaking forefinger at the colonel.

"Sorry to be here on such an errand, Colonel." The sheriff was well known to Silver Birches. "This man's claimin' you are harborin' his property."

"If you're referrin' to Miss Lucy Anne, she's not here. I've questioned my slaves. Seems Zeke brought her some message from her daddy. She probably went on home." The colonel carelessly flicked off the heads of a few wilted flowers nearby.

"She isn't there. Simmons is dead with a bullet through his head."

All the anger and pain of Silver's leaving, the disgust with Simmons for not staying alive and taking care of his daughter, the festering wound that had grown since Frank's departure, culminated in the colonel's cold order, "Then I suggest you arrest this man for murder, instead of chasin' some girl around the countryside." He fixed his steely blue eyes on the man. "How d'we know he's even who he claims to be? He says he holds mortgages on the Simmons place. Simmons is dead and can't speak for himself. Are we to take this man's word against that of a friend and neighbor?"

Reynolds lunged for the colonel. A pistol had appeared in his hand.

"Here, none of that!" The sheriff grabbed the pistol. He turned back to the colonel, almost regretfully. "It's true, all right. We found papers in Simmons's desk showin' he'd signed notes, and they were all overdue. He's also got duly witnessed papers to take

146

Lucy Anne, claimin' nearest of kin."

"Well, she isn't here."

"Ask his granddaughter where she is," Reynolds spat out.

"I guess we'll have to question Miss Silver, Colonel. Will you call her, please?" The sheriff squirmed, showing how he hated what he was being forced to do.

"She's — away. On a visit." The colonel's eyes never left the sheriff.

"Left mighty sudden like, now didn't she, Colonel?" Malevolent eyes matched the glare in Colonel Trevelyan's. "I reckon we'll just have a look around."

"Hold it." The sheriff stepped between the two. "If Colonel Trevelyan's tellin' us she ain't here, then that's good enough for me." He eyed Reynolds. "You got a right to go after the Simmons girl. You ain't got a right to bother Miss Silver."

"When she's caught helpin' a slave escape, then we'll see how many rights I've got." Reynolds stalked off the covered porch.

"She isn't even with Lucy Anne." Not by the movement of a single muscle did the colonel betray his personal suspicions. "Silver left me a note tellin' me she was leavin'. There was no word about Lucy Anne."

Reynolds' eyes glittered with hate. "Then how come Lucy Anne's horse Calico's in your stable, along with that big black Sultan everyone in the county knows is never ridden by anyone but your granddaughter?"

"Is that true?" the sheriff demanded.

"I'll find out." The colonel led the way through the still-falling rain to the stables. "Boy, did you put Sultan or Calico up?"

The stable hand's teeth flashed wide. "Sho' did. Found them standin' outside the stable when I cum this mawnin'." His smile faded. "Funny, tho', how they got out."

"Nothin' funny about it," the colonel declared and turned away as if it were all settled. "Silver rode to Lexington and dropped Lucy Anne at home. When Silver got there, she turned Sultan loose and he came home, just like. . . ." He couldn't finish the sentence, but savagely turned on Reynolds. "Are you satisfied?"

"No!" His insolence stopped the colonel short. "Your little story doesn't allow for how Calico got back here."

"How should I know?" The colonel stepped out of the stable. "Maybe she got loose."

"And maybe she didn't."

"Are you callin' me a liar?" The colonel's very quietness was threatening.

"I'm just sayin' that there's some queer thin's goin' on, and I aim to get my property."

"Massa," the stable hand had followed them out. "I 'most fo'got to tell yo', thos' hosses wuzn't wearin' no saddles."

"What?" The colonel glared at the boy.

"No, suh. They wuz free's when they wuz bo'n."

Reynolds shouted with triumph. "I told you somethin' rotten was goin' on. C'mon, Sheriff, we've got two gals to find." He ran to where the horses were tethered.

"Sorry, Colonel, but looks like he's right." The sheriff took one look at the grim-faced man and turned away. "Mount up, fellers, looks like we got a plum' distast'ful job ahead."

Grimacing, he mounted and rode away, but not before Reynolds called back, "I aim to get even with you, Colonel, if it's the last thin' on earth I do."

His taunt roused the colonel. "You try anythin', and it will be!" His ire reached new heights. "If ever you set foot on my land again, I'll shoot you down the way I would a mad dog." His only answer was a maniacal burst of laughter.

Colonel Trevelyan tottered to the house, brushing off the concerned attentions of

Mammy and the stable hand.

"But my chile, whar she is?" Mammy cried.

A dull glaze settled over the Colonel's pain-filled face. "God only knows, Mammy, God only knows." He wove to the well-stocked liquor cabinet, kept for his guests rather than himself. Pouring out a large measure of the burning liquid, he drank deeply, ignored the heat in his throat, and drank again. In the next hour he continued to drink. So this was what came of respecting God, trying to raise his grandchildren as true Virginians and southerners! Frank turned traitor. Silver refusing to marry a fine gentleman, swayed by wicked gossip.

Hours later he staggered to his room, fell insensible on his bed, bitterness overruling all else. For the first time in years there was no Bible reading. God had forsaken him. Why should he read or pray? But as sleepless minutes ticked far into the night, he came to himself. What had he done? For an awful moment it was as if he were facing God Himself, meeting accusing eyes. Had *he* been to blame? Had he driven them away for living up to what they felt was right, the way he had taught them? Silver had told him that was what Frank had done. Now she was gone, too.

"God forgive me!" The cry burst from a tortured soul. The chill that had been over him slowly left. The first peace he had known since Frank left claimed him.

Sometime later he awoke, breathing heavily, coughing. Why was the room so smoky? Had that fool boy used wet wood? Why was there a fire in the fireplace this time of year, anyway? He leaped from bed, ran to the hall. The smoke was thicker here.

Fire! Silver Birches was on fire.

"Fire!" His stentorian voice rang through the great home. "Mammy. Jasmine. Luke." He frantically pounded on doors, coughing. A burst of sound from outside told him the slave quarters had been roused. Shouts and running feet were followed by pounding on the door. Mammy ran from her room.

"Are any of the other servants in the house?"

"No. Jes' me."

"Get out, Mammy." He sagged against the wall, nearly overcome with smoke, knees buckling.

"Not wifout yo', suh." Fear lent super-human strength to the big Negro woman. She half carried, half dragged him down the great staircase. The great door flew open. Half a dozen slaves swarmed in, seizing them with strong hands, helping them to safety.

Already buckets of water were being passed from hand to hand. Grimy faces and dirty hands were streaked with tears. Here and there a face stood out, a face that had no sorrow. Jasmine's lip curled as if in satisfaction, even as she helped. One or two others, the new acquisitions, smiled. But the colonel never saw them.

"Get the horses from the stables," he commanded, forcing himself to hobble away from the burning house. "They'll go next."

Uneasy daylight showed havoc. In spite of the bucket brigade and the rain now turning still-smoking timbers into grim reminders, Silver Birches was gone. Only a small portion at one end had escaped. The stables were safe. The slave quarters were safe. Colonel Trevelyan and his slaves stood silently before the ruin.

"How — how could it have started?" the colonel asked.

There was no immediate answer. But a search showed a few smouldering rags. Luke silently brought them for inspection.

"Kerosene!" The colonel whispered. "Someone deliberately fired Silver Birches." His eyes ran the ranks of his servants. Had one of them — no! It was too monstrous to consider.

"I aim to get even." The malicious words swam into the colonel's brain. "Reynolds!" Some of his old fire and spunk revived him. "That trash has fired Silver Birches." He turned his face from the travesty of a home before him. "God forgive him — and help him if ever I lay my hands on him!"

He was scarcely conscious that concerned neighbors had come, alarmed by the strange red glow that could be seen for miles away, highlighting the sky like a great painting. Expressions of sympathy didn't even register. He sagged against the side of the carriage they brought him, vaguely aware of being taken to someone's plantation.

"You can see about rebuildin' tomorrow," someone said.

I can never regain that which is lost. Had he spoken aloud? No, the friends would have responded. Lost in his misery, too proud to let them see how his lips trembled, filled with regrets about Frank and Silver, a beaten old man was taken away from his beloved land. It wasn't until they neared their destination that he realized he was still clutching the one thing he'd snatched unconsciously as he fled the burning mansion. Not his cane, symbol of authority, but his old Bible.

From the safety of a nearby thicket, a man

watched with satisfaction. The sheer despair of proud Colonel Trevelyan, the ruined, smoking mansion where he had been so mistreated, the wails of the slaves as they wearily sought rest in their own quarters, were sweet to his senses. It had been worth agreeing to call off the hunt until morning, as the sheriff suggested. He had established his alibi early by announcing he would ride into Lexington and see if there was any trace of the girls. In full view of the wet posse, he had headed that way.

It had been an easy matter to turn and circle, once out of view of the men. The rain would obliterate his departure from the main road and cover every sign of what he was going to do.

Now it was over, and he rejoiced, wickedness evident in every carved line of his cruel face. Tomorrow he would find Lucy Anne Simmons and Silver Trevelyan. When he did, neither would be spared. His heart pounded in anticipation. His mind planned and rejected. At last he had it. If they found the girls' trail, he would suggest they separate. He would be the one to get to them first, and when he did. . . . His fist clenched, crushing the delicate leaf he had plucked, and a laugh of sheer exultance split the early-morning air.

18

A vagrant ray of light stole through the narrow opening where Silver slept, with Lucy Anne a dead weight in her arms. She stirred restlessly, shivered with cold, and thought crossly, *Why hasn't Mammy started a fire?*

She slowly opened her eyes, unable to grasp where she was. Lucy Anne's tumbled curls on her lap roused her. Everything from the night before swept through her.

"Lucy Anne, wake up." Silver shook her.

How vulnerable Lucy Anne looked! Her brown eyes opened wide, and she smiled at Silver; then dawning realization of reality drove the smile away, leaving pain.

"We have to plan what to do." For the first time Silver was uncertain.

"Then it really isn't a nightmare." Lucy Anne sat up, clutching Frank's jacket around her.

"No." Silver slipped to the opening and peered out. "It's still raining, but not so hard." She fumbled in one of the packs and drew out cold biscuits and ham, pilfered from the kitchens. "Here."

"What I'd give for a drink of water!"

"I'm afraid we'll be seein' a lot of water

155

before we're through," Silver said soberly. She drew out the precious map. "Lucy Anne, we'd better both memorize this then destroy it. I wouldn't want to get anyone else in trouble."

"Silver," Lucy Anne steadied her lips. "How can we travel by the North Star, if it rains?"

"It won't keep it up, silly. This is August. Once the storm blows by, we'll get sunshine and clear nights." She tapped the map. "All we do is go straight north. If we have to change directions to get past a town, then we have to get back headed north."

Lucy Anne squinted at the almost illegible writing. "How far is it?"

"About a hundred and twenty-five miles." Silver ignored Lucy Anne's exclamation of dismay. "We can do it; we have to." She forced a smile. "Haven't you always wanted to pioneer it, the way our grandparents did?"

"Not with Reynolds chasin' me." The next instant Lucy Anne was contrite. "I'm sorry. I shouldn't have said that. If it weren't for me, you'd be safe at home."

Silver turned on her, voice savage: "For once and for all, Lucy Anne Simmons, I'm not here just because of you. I'd already made up my mind to run away if worst came to worst about Taylor. We're in this together, and don't you forget it!"

Laughter rippled from Lucy Anne, the last thing Silver would have expected. "I must say, our little 'vacation' sure hasn't done anythin' toward improvin' your temper!"

Silver's mouth curved in an unwilling smile. No one could resist Lucy Anne's sparkling mirth, even if she did have a dirty face and tossed short curls. "It won't be so bad. Frank said he'd make it in a week or ten days. We ought to make it in two weeks at the most." She repacked their gear into two packs, unobtrusively putting most of the food in Lucy Anne's pack, the heavier blankets and extra warm clothing in her own.

"Ready, pioneer?"

"How are you goin' to get to the river without leavin' tracks?"

Silver's optimism died. "I don't know." She stared around the little dirty room that had suddenly became a haven. "There's nothin' here to help us. Just a bunch of rotten gunnysacks." She kicked them in distaste.

"That's it." Lucy Anne was already separating them. "We can wrap them over our boots." Her face flushed as her delicate fingers wrapped and tied.

"I feel like I'm walkin' on boxes," Silver

complained. "But they'll not give us away."
The sacks had been in such poor condition
it took several layers to keep them on.
"Ready?"

The plantation was silent as they slipped
into the misty day. Once Lucy Anne
glanced in the direction of the only home
she had ever known, then set her face north
and trudged after Silver. In spite of the rain,
the river was still low, and they crossed it
easily, although Silver slipped on a rock
once and nearly went down. Even after they
got across, they waded upstream for what
seemed like hours. Only when Lucy Anne
gave signs of exhaustion, would Silver agree
to getting out of the water and resting in a
nearby thicket.

"Well, so far, we're doin' fine."

"I wonder if they've found Daddy yet."
Lucy Anne blinked. "Or if Reynolds has
come and gone to Silver Birches."

"Not much chance he hasn't. At least
we're away." She put the burlap pieces back
on her feet and motioned Lucy Anne to do
the same. "It's hard walkin' with these, but
at least until we get farther away, we'd
better."

By the time darkness fell, the two girls had
covered a good distance. Once they'd heard
the baying of hounds in the distance. Sil-

ver's quick gasp was faithfully reflected by Lucy Anne, but the hounds must have been after a rabbit. Their baying dwindled in the distance, and the girls could breathe again. Shuffling along in their improvised foot coverings, Silver even managed to coax a smile or two out of her friend. "If Taylor Randolph could see me now, he'd decide mighty quick he didn't want me."

"Oh, I don't know." Lucy Anne considered the unusual color in Silver's white skin brought on by exertion. "You're really kind of cute with short curls and a red face."

"And you're simply stunnin' with your dirty face and hands," Silver retorted.

"Do you think we should have used that lamp black and made our faces dark?"

Silver slowly shook her head. "N-no. I thought of it, but two Negro boys would be more noticeable than two white boys." Contrition filled her face. "I didn't mean that!"

"It's all right." There was no hurt in Lucy Anne's face. "I've been white so long I can't get used to the idea the law says I'm not. I don't feel any different. Why does what some men say make me different?"

"It doesn't." But the conversation had given Silver an idea. Stooping, she scooped up a handful of rich black Virginia earth, then shut her eyes hard and rubbed dirt all over her face.

"Silver Trevelyan!" Nothing she had done so far had shocked Lucy Anne so much, yet she followed Silver's lead, and moments later, two filthy-faced boys with dirty hands giggled their way into the trees adjacent to the road.

It was well they had disguised themselves when they did. A light buggy turned into the old path they had thought disused. "Here, you dirty boys! Get outta my way." An arrogant driver swept past. "Don't know what this state's comin' to, boys like that runnin' around this time of night when they should be home doin' chores." His complaints drifted back even after he rounded the bend.

An impish smile lighted Lucy Anne's dirty face. "How come we ain't doin' chores?"

Catching her attempt to lighten their danger, Silver fell in with their phony speech. "We-all is goin' fishin'. No mo' chores for us!"

Their laughter and high spirits lasted until they crept together for the night. In spite of the warm day, the evening was chill. They shared the blankets and huddled without a fire. "Soon as we get far enough away, we'll have a fire," Silver promised.

"It's all right." The long day's tramp was already telling on Lucy Anne. She was asleep in minutes. A protective stirring inside Silver tightened her arms about her friend. Was this how a mother felt? Silver seemed to have aged, along with the rest of them. If only her own mother had lived, how different things might have been.

Resentment against the colonel rose then ebbed away. In spite of everything, he was her grandfather, and she loved him.

Silver fell asleep but, while it was still dark, awoke cramped. She hated rousing Lucy Anne, but she must. Even the miles they had covered the day before wouldn't insure their safety.

After the first struggle to waken, Lucy Anne came alive without complaint. She obediently rubbed more dirt on her face to replace what had come off on Silver's clothing during the night hours. Before dawn they were back on the road, this time using the main track. No one would be along this time of night. Even if someone came, they could easily slip into the clumps of laurel at the side of the road.

"Someone's comin'." The low whisper roused Silver from her thoughts. They dashed from the road. Faint daylight showed a horseman plodding along the road. Try as she would, she couldn't make out his face.

"Is it Reynolds?" Stark terror shone in Lucy Anne's eyes.

"No. Too short, from what you've told me of him." Crouched among the big leaves, they watched him pass. The sound of slow hoof beats and the creaking of saddle leather disappeared.

It was only the first of many times they would crouch in the best available cover. Silver lost track of days after the first three or four. They were so alike! Endless trudging. Fear. Stumbling. Day and night blending. Rain ceasing. Stars pouring out welcome light. It was easier on the starry nights. They could follow the North Star and then sleep days, well hidden. There had been no sign of Reynolds.

A few things fell into routine. Automatically they removed their now-worn gunnysack pads when they came to creeks and branches, then waded until the water swirled and eddied around their feet.

"I wonder how many miles we've waded," Lucy Anne asked one early evening. Her face had thinned until her cheekbones stuck out, giving her a hunted look. Silver knew her own face was no rounder. Yet Lucy

Anne never complained.

"If I remember the map, we must be in the new state now."

"Does that mean we're safe?"

Silver looked at her in pity. "Neither of us are safe. State lines don't mean anythin' to the law."

Lucy Anne cried out, for the first time, "Will I ever be free and safe again?" She held out a thin arm. "Are we really goin' to make it?" She sank to a stone, weeping bitterly.

"We are goin' to make it." Silver drove her teeth in her lip. "You're just worn out. No wonder, after fallin' in the river this mornin'."

"And losin' most of what little food we've got left." Remorse tangled with Lucy Anne's sobbing. "I'm just so tired, it seems as if I could drop down here and die."

Determination gave Silver the strength to order, "You stay hidden. I'm goin' to see if I can't find someplace where we can make a fire and get you dried out to the skin." She frowned as Lucy Anne coughed. "Can't have you gettin' sick."

"I'm not sick, just tired." Lucy Anne leaned her head back on the big rock and closed her eyes. But an hour later, when Silver returned with news she'd located a small cave nearby, Lucy Anne was burning with fever.

It was the beginning of horror for Silver. Nothing in life had prepared her to care for anyone sick. A dozen times she cried silently, *If only Mammy were here!* She thought wildly of finding a doctor and gave it up immediately. They hadn't come all this way to be found out and dragged back. The fires Mammy had tended haunted Silver as she struggled with a pitifully inadequate blaze. Yet her determination matched her lack of skill. Over and over she tried until she had a fire going at the mouth of the little cave. She managed to heat water and add tea and some dried meat. The broth was strengthening. Lucy Anne gulped it when told to, then fell back to her blankets. Her cough continued.

Why hadn't she packed medicine? Silver scourged herself. Hard on the thought came another: even if she had, she might have killed Lucy Anne by not knowing what to give her or when. For the very first time, Silver realized how useless she really was. Girls on other plantations were taught such things. Not Silver. She had rebelled against what she called "woman's work," and the colonel laughed and gave in to her. Outside of her superb riding skills and dabbling with music and painting, there wasn't one single thing she could do well.

"If I ever get Lucy Anne to safety, I'm goin' to learn how to care for sick folks and how to cook and make good fires." She gritted her teeth. Then, "I don't know any more if you're a southerner, or a northerner, God, but please, help Lucy Anne." To her inexperienced touch, Lucy Anne was as hot as ever. She poured cold water on a piece of Frank's shirttail she'd ripped off and placed it on the burning forehead.

Worst of all, they were nearly out of food. What could she do? Had she encouraged Lucy Anne to run away from persecution only to die in the hills? "No!" she told the North Star that had appeared in the dusk. "I won't let it happen."

Something moved in the bushes. Silver turned to stone. The next instant a loud "Mooo" filled the air, then a call, "Soo — ee." Silver shooed the cow away from the cave, being careful to keep hidden. Her heart lurched then beat hard. Racing back to the cave, she snatched up the big tin cup she shared with Lucy Anne. Did she dare carry out her plan? A moan from Lucy Anne convinced her. She had to. Step by cautious step she followed the cow, then the cow's owner, until they reached a crude stable with a small house nearby. The farmer lighted a lantern, and its rays illuminated a kindly face. Silver weighed it and took a deep breath, then stepped into the circle of light where the man was milking the cow.

"Evenin'."

The farmer whirled on his three-legged stool. "Evenin' to you. Out purty late, ain't you, boy?" He peered at Silver. "You be those new folks in the neighborhood?"

It was the perfect opening. Silver hitched her britches nonchalantly up. "I be." She swaggered to the man. "Kin I buy a drink o' milk?"

"Shore." He held out a brown hand for her cup. "No charge. Neighbor's meant fer helpin' neighbor."

His kindness sent a lump to Silver's throat. She pulled her cap down lower and extended the cup, greedily watching the rich milk foam into it.

"There. Better git on, young feller, it's mighty dark."

"I'm obliged." She turned away, careful not to spill even one drop.

"Yore a funny feller." The farmer's comment stopped her dead still.

"How come?"

"Tho't youda drunk it up right here."

Silver frantically searched for an explanation and drawled, "Got a piece to go. I'm savin' it." Before he could say more she hurried into the darkness. Every nerve and muscle cried out, *run*, but she forced herself to whistle, thankful Frank had taught her long ago, and saunter away, making sure she kept the stable between them. Once she was out of earshot she hurried as fast as she could without spilling it. She could almost taste it. She'd never been hungrier for anything, she who despised milk! Yet sight of Lucy Anne's pale face from which the fever had subsided changed Silver's mind. She carefully portioned the milk, allowing Lucy Anne to drink only half of it. The rest she put aside for the morning. She dared not go back for more, and Lucy Anne needed it worse than she did.

"You drink the rest," the wan girl insisted.

"I drank my fill at the farmhouse," Silver lied, extremely conscious of the milk's strong attraction. When Lucy Anne leaned back, a little more color filled her face, but it was natural. The fever had broken.

Which had done it? Had God helped Lucy Anne in answer to Silver's prayer? Or was it the milk? Had God sent the cow so there would be milk? Sudden longing to throw it all into God's lap, if He had one, and get rid of her awesome responsibility washed over Silver. She was so tired, and it seemed so far to Harmony.

She had lied to Lucy Anne. She had begged from the farmer. What else would she have to do before this horrible experience was over? God surely wouldn't answer the prayers of a liar and beggar. She tossed on the hard ground of the cave, struggling against the wash of regret that attacked when she was weakest. The only sure thing was that they had so far escaped. It couldn't be more than a few more days' travel to Harmony.

The next morning, Lucy Anne's silent pleading, when she drained the tin cup, gave Silver added boldness. She'd march right back down to that farmer and get more. She followed her plan until she reached the edge of the little clearing in the woods. Every sense sharpened, she stepped from behind an oak and stood motionless. A horse with reins drooping stood in front of the little house. Was it the farmer's?

The door opened. Silver peered through her lacy curtain of leaves. Morning sun shone bright on something pinned to a man's shirt.

It was a silver badge.

Cold sweat stood out on Silver's forehead.

Across the clearing came the hearty voice of the farmer, "Like I said, no one's bin here 'cept a boy askin' for a drink o' milk. If'n I see two gals I'll holler."

"Thanks." The officer mounted and rode past Silver's tree, so close she could have reached out and touched him.

Silver sank to the ground. Her first impulse to flee was stifled by realization they were safer here than anywhere, at least for the present. The farmer would find out she wasn't a neighbor boy, but it would take time.

All thought of asking for more milk died. She mustn't be seen again. Although the farmer had been kind, he was powerless to stop the law.

She didn't tell Lucy Anne. There was no use. Until the younger girl was better, they couldn't travel. But she did lie in the bushes near the pasture for hours. The cow would come, and if she could, she would get more milk for Lucy Anne.

It was a struggle. Even patient Sukie could sense Silver's total lack of knowledge. It took several tries, but finally Silver had her reward. Just before the farmer came calling his cow, Silver triumphantly carried a brimming cup of milk to the cave. Silver had added theft to her list of sins.

For three evenings she fought inexperience and was rewarded with milk for Lucy Anne. Never did she drink a drop herself. She satisfied herself with a bit of cornbread that was now getting moldy around the edges and cold water from a nearby branch.

At last Lucy Anne was able to travel again, but more slowly. They stood in the road and cried when they saw a sign telling a disinterested world it was just ten miles to Harmony.

"We really are goin' to make it," Lucy Anne panted, after a sprint that drained them both. She threw her arms around Silver. "We'll be there late tonight!"

Apprehension touched Silver. Was it an intuitive warning or merely her reaction to hunger? She'd given Lucy Anne the last of their food that morning. Now weakness threatened to undo everything.

Ahead was a tumbledown shack. Lucy Anne eyed it longingly. "Could we stop there, just to rest for a little while?"

Silver scanned the country around them. No sign of life and not much cover. "I think it would be safe." Her eyes lit on a forsaken orchard. New strength flowed into her veins. "Lucy Anne, there are blackberries!"

They flew to the bushes, stripping them,

stuffing them in their mouths until the juice flew. The berries were past their prime, but never had anything tasted better. What they couldn't eat, Silver put in her battered cup and took inside. They would have something before starting their last few miles of the long journey.

"Is it safe to wash our faces now?" Lucy Anne looked at Silver in disgust. "Am I as seedy lookin' as you are?"

"Worse," Silver assured her. Her dark eyes twinkled. "Of course, it's more important for you to look nice than me. I'm only meetin' a brother, and you're meetin' a sweetheart."

"I wouldn't be too sure of that," Lucy Anne taunted. "Seems I remember a red-headed visitor —"

What she was going to say was lost in the drum of hootbeats.

"Get inside, Lucy Anne!" Silver dragged her through the doorless opening.

"They aren't comin' here!"

Silver peered out. "Yes, they are." Her heart sank. The horse leading the band of men was unfamiliar, but even through the dusk, she recognized the second horse as having been in front of the farmer's place while she hid nearby.

Lips close to Lucy Anne's ear, she

breathed, "No matter what you see, *don't make a single sound.*" Her glance roved the filthy shack, lit on the cupful of berries. Smashing a few through her fingers, she dabbed her face until it was spotted and to Lucy Anne's horror, stepped out the doorway and ran across the yard.

She was a good fifty yards from the tumbling shack when the lead horseman spotted her. Never had she seen such cruel eyes. She abandoned her flight and turned and ran toward him. It had to be Reynolds. Thank God he'd never seen her.

"Help me, oh, somebody help me!" Her eerie cry shattered the gathering night.

"Who? What — ?" Reynolds reined in, penetrating the gloom. "Boy, what's wrong with you?"

God, if You really care at all, help. Silver's silent prayer winged skyward through the night. "Help me. My folks died. In there." She pointed to the brooding building.

"Whatsa matter?" The sheriff pulled up by Reynolds. "What're them spots on your face?"

"Fever." Silver moaned. "Dead. They're all dead." She added a morbid laugh. It rang crazily in the waiting silence.

With an oath, Reynolds spurred his horse into a great leap. "Let's get out of here! I ain't catchin' no sickness."

"We can't just leave the boy," the sheriff protested, even as his horse backed nervously.

"Send the doc at Harmony back. The folks're dead. He will be too, from the looks of it."

"Makes sense, Sheriff. We don't want no epidemic started," a voice called out, followed by agreement from the others.

Silver laughed again, shrill, unnatural, and finished with a gurgle in her throat. It was enough to convince the sheriff. "You stay here. I'll send the doc."

"Dead, dead, dead," she croaked. Returning courage even gave her the ability to raise one hand and point to the shack. "Dead."

A horse nickered. A man swore. Hoofbeats pounded in the night. No sooner had they disappeared than Lucy Anne ran into the overgrown yard. In the light of the moon just scouting over a low hill nearby, she appeared made of snow. "It was Reynolds." A wild little laugh not unlike Silver's own bubbled from her throat. "Did he track us here?"

"More likely he figured out where we were headin' and came to wait for us." Silver flopped to a log, drained. Not for long, "We're goin' to make it, Lucy Anne, if you'll do exactly as I tell you." In a whisper she outlined what lay ahead and what Lucy Anne had to do.

11

"It all depends on whether Dr. Stuart brings anyone with him," Silver said. Lucy Anne's ice-cold hands touched Silver's arm, but she made no sound. "When we hear them comin', or anyone, you must crawl in the bunk and pull that old blanket over your head. If worst comes to worst, I'll tell them you're dead."

Lucy Anne gasped, glanced at the dirty bunk and blanket, then straightened her slim shoulders. "I'll do whatever you tell me."

"Now, we'll sit here and wait until someone comes." Silver dropped to the doorsill and leaned against the jamb. She stretched her eyes wide to keep sheer fatigue from closing them. Lucy Anne settled beside her, huddled as they had done every night on the journey. Her still-cold hands felt like an icy river against Silver's feverishly alert arms.

Silver moistened parched lips, tasting blood. In spite of pouring water into herself until she sometimes thought she'd drown, her mouth was sore, her lips cracked. "Lucy Anne," she hesitated, wondering if she

175

could say what she must without crying. "I just want you to know — I love you more than any sister I ever dreamed of havin'." She heard a little choked sob but ploughed on. "I don't know what may happen. We may make it, but then we may not. No matter what's ahead, I just wanted you to know."

Lucy Anne couldn't answer. She just pressed her tear-wet face into Silver's dirty jacket and sobbed, her arms tight around her friend. The moment of closeness stretched to two, then three. In spite of Silver's determination to be alert when riders came, she felt herself nodding.

Was it minutes or hours later that her eyes flew open. "Lucy Anne, riders are comin'!"

Incredibly, Lucy Anne was wide awake instantly. Without a word she squeezed Silver's arm and ran for the dirty bunk. The next instant she was prone, covered into a seemingly lifeless mound under a travel-stained blanket.

Two riders swept into the weed-infested yard, to the shack. "Someone sick here?"

The stiffening in Silver's knees gave way to relief. It was Zachary Stuart. There was no mistaking his crisp voice in a land of southern accents.

He swung from the saddle easily and

stepped to the doorway, where Silver supported herself against the crumbling frame. "What's all this about an epidemic?" He peered into Silver's face.

Torn between wanting to cry out and fear that the second man now dismounting might be the sheriff, Silver could only stand in the shadow.

"Come out and let me take a look at you, boy." Firm hands drew her from her haven, tipped her head back. Her cap fell off and revealed the short dark curls and the terrified face in the pitiless moonlight.

Dr. Stuart recoiled. "Miss Trevelyan!"

"Silver." Frank's muffled shout echoed in the still night. He ran to her, brushing his larger friend aside as if he had been a troublesome horsefly. "Silver, it's really you?" His eyes swept her from head to toe, then peered into the shadows back of her. "Is —" he licked his lips. "Is Lucy Anne . . . ?" Dread filled his face.

A rush of flying feet was his answer. Silver held her breath as Lucy Anne, still dragging the old blanket, pushed into the group. This was the moment she had dreaded. As one in a dream she saw Lucy Anne step close to Frank and look into his face. Frank's arms opened, but Lucy Anne held herself rigid.

"I'm not what you think I am, Frank."

The pain of every step of the long trek to freedom distorted her features.

Again Silver held her breath. *Frank, please Frank.* . . . Her silent plea was unnecessary.

"You are everything I think you are and more." The steady eyes of the boy turned man had nothing to hide. The next moment Lucy Anne was sobbing in his arms.

"Come." Dr. Stuart gently led Silver away, leaving the two together in their joy too private to be shared.

"Then you know?"

His eyes sought hers in the moonlight. "We've known for days. Reynolds came and told us, raving like a madman. We've watched and prayed, unable to seek for you when you were long overdue, because we knew we were also being watched. Only threat of sickness kept us free tonight." He gently touched the spots on her face. "Blackberry?"

"Yes." Silver's heart was filled to overflowing. "I didn't think Frank would still be here."

"He would have pushed on, but he was pretty well tuckered when he arrived. By the time he rested, the grapevine had it the colonel wasn't going to pursue him, so he stayed here and has been helping me."

"I can't go back — ever." It washed over

Silver more clearly than it had done even in the black hours of her flight.

"Miss Trevelyan," the strong hands holding her shoulders also seemed to be holding up her world. "Can you be strong?"

"Yes," she whispered, mind a jumble. Did he mean there was a warrant for her arrest? Or that Lucy Anne could still be taken?

"There's nothing to go back to." Compassion filled his face. "Silver Birches burned to the ground the night after you left."

A vision of the proud home danced before her eyes. "What about my grandfather?" A sharp thrust of fear hoarsened her voice.

"He only lived a few days. I suspect Reynolds fired the place. His eyes showed his satisfaction."

Silver didn't hear. "Then it's *my* fault." Hot tears poured. "I killed the colonel."

"Stop it!" The shake he administered was far from gentle. "The truth came out. He had had a heart problem for years but never told anyone. The shock of the fire was too much. The neighbors who took him home said he just sat and stared and read the Bible, the only thing he'd saved. When they chided him about rebuilding, he only smiled." He bit off words, as if reluctant to continue. "His last words were, 'Tell Silver — and Frank —' "

"Go on," Silver ordered, hands clenching over his strong arm.

" 'Tell them I leave legacy. . . .' It was all."

"Then he never forgave us." Her voice was curiously flat, as if everything had proved to be too much to comprehend. "Our legacy is fear and hate and knowing we helped speed his death."

"It is not!" His drawn face shone with honesty. "He dropped his hands to his lap where the Bible lay. I believe with every ounce of my being he was trying to show he did forgive you and that your legacy was more than Silver Birches."

"If I can only believe that!" Her pitiful cry echoed in the night. She pressed both hands to her throbbing temples. "Oh, what a difference it will make if I can believe that."

"You can." Frank's solemn voice whirled her toward him. "I do."

With an inarticulate cry, Silver hurled herself into her brother's arms. He just let her cry, but when she settled down a bit, he said, "Since I've been here, I've learned what forgiveness really is. It's not just sayin' you're sorry and havin' someone say it's all right." His lips quirked in a smile. "I've learned our real legacy is from a different source. It's our Heavenly Father who gives it."

"I never heard you talk like this before," Silver told him.

"I never before knew the Lord Jesus Christ. Since I've asked him to forgive my sins and be my traveling companion, the whole world's different."

Silver looked at him with wondering eyes. "On the trip, I tried to pray, and the cow came, and. . . ."

"Wait." Dr. Stuart lifted his hand. The sound of hoofbeats neared, then disappeared in the distance. He took a deep breath. "Silver, Lucy Anne, there's something you must know."

What now? Silver felt as if she could bear no more.

Lucy Anne's eyes stood big and staring in her thin face. "What is it, Dr. Stuart?" She nestled in the crook of Frank's protecting arm.

"We have to start toward Canada. Tonight." Frank's eyes grew suspiciously moist as he looked at the weary girl. For one moment only she sagged, then straightened. "All right."

It was Silver who protested, memory of

Lucy Anne's weakness filling her. "She can't. She's been sick. She has to rest first." Yet even as she spoke she knew it was inevitable. For this she had brought Lucy Anne to Harmony. Shrugging off her dread of the coming journey, she said, "When do we start?"

Frank exchanged glances with Dr. Stuart, who said, "Not you, Silver."

"What do you mean?"

"You can't go with them. The law is looking for two girls. You'd only add to their danger. They won't be looking for a man and a girl. We've already gotten clothing and food together. Frank knows how to contact people at different points. They'll get through."

"You can't ask me to let Lucy Anne go," she cried, fear and frustration overflowing. "After what we've gone through together, I just can't —" She choked.

"You can and will. Your love for Lucy Anne and Frank must be big enough to let them go."

Silver slowly turned to Lucy Anne. How could she permit her to go on? Yet what if she insisted on going with them and because of it Reynolds caught Lucy Anne? She closed her eyes tight, then opened them. "Good-bye, Lucy Anne."

The younger girl ran to her. Clung to her. Suffering gave way to acceptance. Frank gently removed her holding fingers. "Someday, Silver. . . ."

It was the same promise he'd given at Silver Birches. Silver turned away blindly, unwilling to see them leave. She could hear the creak of saddle leather, then galloping hooves. She turned. She was alone in the clearing with Dr. Stuart.

"What will become of me?"

"Do you need to ask that?"

Silver had the sense of being drawn slowly into a net of safety. Yet he hadn't moved.

"My parents will welcome you. Later, after you've rested, if you want to help about the house or in my work, there will be a place for you."

His words rang in her ears as they double mounted his horse and picked their way back to Harmony. Peace lay over the small village like a mantle. She shivered, thinking of Frank and Lucy Anne with so many miles to go! Once she asked, "How will they get there?"

"It's better you don't know." The calm voice steadied her. The slow gait of the horse lulled her as they left the borders of the village and traveled on.

"Wake up, Silver. We're home." Zachary

Stuart lifted her from the horse.

Home! Her sleep-blurred eyes took in a house ahead. A barking dog ran toward them. A dim light in a window beckoned her. Somehow she managed to stumble into the house. A sweet-faced, white-haired woman and a man who looked strangely like Dr. Stuart greeted her. She forced herself to eat what was given her. Then Mrs. Stuart led her to a spotless room, helped her wash, and put her into a bed. After her nights on the ground, Silver nearly cried out at the softness.

"Father, we thank Thee for this, our child, who has come to us." The woman kissed Silver's forehead, smoothing back the curls. Then she blew out the lamp and was gone.

Sleep claimed Silver. Not even thought of her brother and Lucy Anne or the colonel could deny the rest her tortured body craved. When she finally awoke, it was with the smell of frying chicken enticingly coaxing her from her deep sleep.

She stretched and looked around her. Everything was white, in contrast to the dirty world she'd been living in. White painted walls and ceillings. Snowy coverlet. White curtains at the sparkling glass windows letting in a flood of sunshine.

She started to get up, groaned, and fell back. That last spurt of travel had been her undoing. Every bone and muscle in her body ached.

"Good morning!" Again Silver was struck by the crisp voice. Mrs. Stuart entered, holding a small tray with a steaming cup of something on it. Silver became aware she was ravenous. "Is that for me?"

"It certainly is. Just a drop of chicken broth to hold you till you're dressed." She propped pillows behind Silver's back and handed her the cup. Nothing had ever tasted so good in all Silver's life.

"The chicken's almost ready. You have time to get up and bathe, if you like. We didn't bother with much last night." Twin dimples flashed in the smooth, rosy cheeks, and the green eyes so like her son's danced.

"I know. I want so much to wash my hair." Silver ruefully looked at the streaked pillowcase where her head had lain.

"We'll give you time. Short as it is, it won't take long to dry on this hot day." She busied herself, straightening items on a high chest of drawers. "You have beautiful hair."

"It used to be." Silver sighed as she caught sight of herself in a mirror.

"It will grow again," Mrs. Stuart told her. "Now, the men will be coming in for lunch soon, so let's get you ready, unless you'd rather have a tray here?"

"No, that's too much trouble." Her eyes unexpectedly brimmed. "You're so kind, takin' me in and all. Do you know about — about me?"

Mrs. Stuart straightened. "Only that you're a poor lost child our Heavenly Father sent here for help." She smiled again. "Isn't that quite a lot?" She didn't wait for an answer but bustled out.

All through her bath and having her hair washed, Silver pondered the answer. Did the woman really believe that? Memory of the change in Frank testified Mrs. Stuart did believe what she had said. A great longing for the unexplainable peace she'd felt last night in Frank, even while he prepared to embark on a journey even more dangerous than her own, had now filled Silver.

"I don't have anythin' fit to wear." Silver sat shrouded in a heavy blanket.

"I have things for you." Mrs. Stuart trotted in and out, carrying garments. "They're plain and a little old-fashioned, but they should fit. You'll put on a few pounds, and they will be fine." She helped Silver into a yellow sprigged-muslin dress over white petticoats.

Silver looked at her curiously. "They are

186

too long for them to have been yours."

"They were our daughter's. Her name was Alicia."

Silver felt a strange reluctance to ask more, but Mrs. Stuart continued, "She died several years ago. She'd have been just about your age. I couldn't bear to give her things away. I'm glad I didn't." Her face softened with memory. "She was a pretty girl, and everyone loved her. But she took pneumonia, and we couldn't save her. It was then Zachary decided to learn about medicine."

Silver's throat tightened. "I just found out about my grandfather."

"I know." Their gazes met in mutual sympathy. "At least we have the comfort of knowing our loved ones belonged to our Father."

Silver averted her gaze from the saintly look on her hostess's face. "How can you be sure?"

"Alicia accepted the Lord as her Saviour and companion when she was a child. Zach tells me your grandfather died holding his Bible and trying to leave a message for you." She stepped back from brushing Silver's short curls into a halo around her face. "There. Anyone seeing you will think you cut your hair because of brain fever or the like."

"Mrs. Stuart." Silver tried twice. "Mrs. Stuart, can anyone have the peace you have and that Frank has found?"

"Of course, child." The wrinkled, workworn hand stroked Silver's soft hair. "We'll be talking more about it. We always read from the Good Book, evenings."

Wistfulness colored Silver's comment. "Frank said our legacy was from our Heavenly Father. What did he mean?" She didn't wait for a reply. "I don't even know God. Why would He leave me a legacy?"

"You may not feel you know Him, but He knows you and loves you."

Remembrance shattered the fragile moment. "Then if He is the lovin' God you say, why am I here? Why is Frank takin' Lucy Anne away?" Tears crowded her eyes. "Wouldn't God stop this war if He cared?" A burst of emotion left her drained. "What does God know about losin' someone you love?"

The stroking hand stilled. "He knows everything, child. He watched His only Son die on a cross."

"And He didn't stop it?" Silver shuddered.

"No. He gave that Son for you and for me, and for all people, that we might live, because Jesus had taken our sins, even though He was innocent." Seeing her confusion, Mrs. Stuart gently added, "It's like what you did. There was no way for your friend to save herself, so you made a sacrifice. You risked punishment for helping her. That's what Jesus did, only on such a greater scale."

That evening Silver sat on the wide porch, which was smaller than the one at Silver Birches, but comfortable. Night sounds reached her: a bird crying, an owl in the distance, rustling of leaves, a frog kerchunking in the pond nearby. Where were Lucy Anne and Frank? Had they safely gotten away? Dr. Stuart had been called out on a visit. The older Stuarts were wisely allowing her to get used to their home.

Seated in the shadows, Silver could still see the yard clearly. Something of the peace of the night stole into her strained senses. It was the first night in weeks she had been able to relax, knowing she was free.

"Hello the house!" The call roused Silver from the stupor she had gradually slipped into. A sickening rush of the same old fear threatened to sweep away all control. The voice was the one she had heard last night — Reynolds, the pursuer.

The front door swung open. A lantern was held high. "Something we can do for you, stranger?"

"Is this the Stuart place?"

"It is."

"Doc home?"

"No." The answer revealed nothing.

"Thought I'd check if he found the sick boy." Reynolds shifted in the saddle and spat a stream of tobacco juice to one side.

"I've seen no boy."

"How about two runaway girls, a Negro slave and the gal who's helpin' her git away from me?" His eyes gleamed red in the lantern light. Silver clutched her breast and put the other hand over her mouth to keep from crying out.

"There are no runaways here, and I've seen no slave. Anything else we can do for you?"

"Naw." Reynolds spat again and wheeled his horse. "Guess mebbe I'm lookin' in the wrong place."

"Mebbe you are." There was a hint of laughter in Mr. Stuart's careful repetition.

A curse and a sound of a falling whip was drowned in the clatter of the horse's spring.

"Miss Trevelyan?" Mr. Stuart peered into Silver's shadowy retreat.

"I'm all right." Her heart started beating full time again.

"He won't be back. Mother and I were wondering if you'd like to come in for a bit of worship now."

"Oh, yes." Thankfully she accepted his arm and courtly help into the house. Inside, she leaned against the doorway to the small, attractive sitting room. "Mr. Stuart, I didn't want you to have to lie for me."

"I didn't, child." He crossed to the mantel and turned the pages of a worn Bible. "The Apostle Paul tells the Galatians, 'There is neither Jew nor Greek, there is neither bond nor free, there is neither male nor female: for ye are all one in Christ Jesus.' " He smiled down at her. "This house has been dedicated to that same Christ Jesus. In it there are no distinctions, and no slaves or runaways, but brothers and sisters in the Lord."

Even though Silver didn't understand all she heard, that worship was indelibly printed in her mind. Again the passionate longing for the thing that made this family what it was seized her in a mighty grip that even her doubts and resentment against God couldn't totally destroy.

12

Months later a bone-weary Silver paused between tasks. The idyll at the Stuart farm hadn't lasted long. Once she regained her superb strength, she demanded to be put to work. Dr. Stuart didn't protest. Silver quickly graduated from kitchen work, ranging from baking bread and scrubbing floors, to assisting the doctor. At first she hated it. The smells and the sickness threatened to nauseate her. In time she learned to control her feelings, and the reward of seeing gratefulness in the eyes of patients overcame her repulsion for the work.

Names she'd never heard before sang in her mind: Carnifix Ferry, Philippi, Romney. A dozen others. Harmony was no longer the peaceful place it had appeared the night she arrived. West Virginia, as the new state was called, was torn with battle. The first time Confederate soldiers were brought to Dr. Stuart's little hospital, she valiantly cared for them, then ran sobbing to a quiet spot under a nearby oak and cried her heart out. The first time a Yankee soldier was brought in, she flinched. She would never care for the enemy!

Yet something in Zach Stuart's green eyes, quiet command, roused in her the obedience needed for them to work together. She approached the bed. Dear God, the boy couldn't be any older than Frank! She bit her lip. Where was the enemy, that dreaded Yankee she'd been taught to hate and fear? It would be as easy to hate Frank as to hate or fear the youngster with pleading eyes and white face. When he died that night, with a whispered thank-you on his lips, Silver trembled as if in shock, then forced herself to draw the blanket over his face.

Dr. Stuart found her crouched under the oak, tearless but distraught. The agony in her face was too much for his iron self-control. He caught her in his arms and held her until her body ceased shaking and a torrent of tears washed away some of her trouble. Not trusting himself to speak, he wiped her face, smiled, and strode back to the sick and dying. It was not the time for what lay in wait.

Over the months she worked at his side, Silver came to respect and admire Dr. Stuart more than anyone she had ever known. When she worked hard, he worked harder. When she went without sleep, he gently forced her to rest, but she never knew if or when he slept.

He is a real man, Silver told herself one evening, when he had fought to save a patient and lost him. "Frank was right. How could anyone help lovin' him?" Yet it was no silly infatuation such as she'd seen other girls develop for "heroes." Her growing regard encompassed far more than his bigness and fearlessness. It went deep into her soul. Sometimes she wondered wistfully if he remembered what he'd said so long ago, over a year now, when he stood with her in the dappled porch of Silver Birches. Never in any way had he referred to it. Yet sometimes she caught his tired eyes on her and noted how they brightened. It was one of the few sunny spots in her suddenly drab life of service.

Another was a sparkling, chatty letter from "Cousin Frances up North," telling how she was taking the veil. Correctly interpreted, it meant Frank and Lucy Anne had made it safely to Canada and were married. Would she ever know what they'd gone through on that final journey? Silver sometimes wondered if she'd ever see them again. War seemed to go on forever.

The brightest spot of all was the Stuart place. They had come from the North years before. That was why they spoke crisply and without dropping their *g's*. They'd home-steaded the place and improved it. They ab-horred slavery and did their own work, aided by paid hired hands, some white, some Negro. Silver began to see the difference in the feeling at the Harmony farm. The Ne-groes still worked hard. They still had their quarters. But the songs they sang were more joyous. She curiously asked Dr. Stuart about it.

"It's because they work *with* us, not for us." His laughing green eyes warmed Silver. "I remember my mother scrubbing floors before she asked Minnie to do it, to show there was nothing wrong with honest labor."

"Then that's why she showed me how!" Silver was enlightened. In spite of her love for Mrs. Stuart, she'd been appalled when given that task.

"Also to show you how to scrub a floor, if ever we lose our place." His face turned somber. "We're far enough back from town that so far we've not been troubled. That doesn't mean we won't be."

Silver's traitorous heart had bounded at "if ever we lose our place." Did he mean her and himself? His following words produced dread. She couldn't stand losing another home, and that's what the Stuart farm had become. She was as familiar with the white room as ever she'd been with the suite at Silver Birches. When she wasn't so dog tired, she was even happy, especially after hearing from Frank and Lucy Anne.

Yet her biggest problem wasn't even lack of sleep or misery over what she saw in her nursing duties. It was God. She just could not reconcile the flaming world around her, the crumbling of everything she'd ever known, with the peace the Stuarts carried and the perfect faith in their Heavenly Father they showed in every day of their lives. Even though she rebelled, she would have given everything she possessed to have it. At times she was so tired she felt she must just give in. Then remembrance of her grandfather's death and the senseless war hardened her heart. Sometimes her life at Silver Birches seemed dreamlike, as if she had never known anything but caring for the wounded. Taylor Randolph's face and his treatment of her blurred. It was so far away.

Fighting was at its thickest by late spring of 1862. Reports of battles across a half-dozen states or more continued to pour in. After a local engagement Silver had the shock of her life. Dr. Stuart had told her a new bunch of wounded were coming in. She hadn't even asked whether they were Yankees or rebels; it no longer mattered. They were just part of a never-ending parade of hurt men to care for and move out to make room for more.

She was moving between beds, her gray gown, under the enveloping white apron, free of hoops, when a low voice stopped her in mid-step. "Miss Silver!"

Who on earth? No one called her anything but "nurse" here. She turned. Feverish eyes peered at her from an emaciated face. Eyes that beseeched her to help, to recognize, in a world gone mad.

"Taylor?" she faltered. She was rewarded by a feeble movement of his right hand, an attempt to salute. It ended in a groan.

Forgetting everything except that he had once been a neighbor, she dropped to her knees by his bedside and touched the crusted hand. "Is it really you?"

"What's left of me."

Where were the arrogant attitude, haughty mien, and proud spirit that once characterized him? Lines of suffering etched his face. A touch of silver at the temples of the blonde hair showed what he had been through.

"So you did get away. Just as well. Nothin' left. It's all gone." Nervous fingers plucked the coverlet. Brooding eyes stared into hers. "They burned my plantation." Great, racking sobs tore him, born of sheer weakness. "Silver, everythin's gone." He touched her hand. "Slaves ran away. Overseer abandoned."

Her heart was wrenched with pity. "You can rebuild."

He shook his head slowly. "I'll never get home."

For a minute his words painted a picture of the way it used to be: Sultan running free, with herself laughing, hairpins flying; the great ballroom filled with laughing, carefree guests; the long tables laden with hickory-cured ham, great roasts of beef, and every kind of vegetable and pie and cake known to cooking. Like a riptide a wash of homesickness covered her, and her hand tightened spasmodically on Taylor's. "Won't it ever be the way it was?"

Her poignant cry roused the sinking captain. Some of the old steel returned to his blue eyes as he said, "Someday, when it's all over, the South will. . . ." He was too weak to go on.

Silver reached for a pitcher, poured water into a cup and forced it between his lips. Even her inexperienced eyes determined there was little more that could be done.

The bandage around his chest was slowly reddening.

"Silver," Taylor's eyes were clear now, but she could see the effort it took for him to speak.

"Hush." Her old, imperious manner bolstered her. "You can talk later."

"No." It came out flat, recognizing later was not for him. "I was rotten, but I did love you. All through the flames and firin', I remembered. Remembered the good times, not all the other." He closed his eyes, then slowly forced them open once more. "It's more than I deserve, but could you —" Shame filled his eyes, and he turned his face away.

Silver understood. She slowly touched his forehead with her lips, noting the chill already replacing the burning fever that had been there earlier.

He never spoke again, merely turned his head toward her, attempted another crooked smile, then closed his eyes.

"Come." A gentle hand led her away.

"He was so different." Silver's trembling fingers clutched Dr. Stuart's sleeve.

"War does that." He placed both hands on her shoulders. "Go home, Silver. Sleep as long as you can. You're nearly dead on your feet."

She obediently stumbled outside. Her faithful pony, Iroquois, nickered from his place beneath the big oak. She was so tired she tried twice before she could mount, then let him find his own way home.

"Why, child, your eyes look like burned holes in a blanket!" Mrs. Stuart greeted her at the door with loving hands. She helped Silver out of her hospital clothing and into a thin nightie, another resurrection from Alicia's wardrobe. She brought hot tea and a sandwich and wouldn't leave until Silver stuffed down every crumb. "Now sleep," she admonished and shut the door to keep out sounds from the rest of the house.

"I don't think I can ever sleep again," Silver whispered. A panorama composed of scenes from Silver Birches, her hospital work, and the trip with Lucy Anne danced on the wall of her mind. Last of all was Taylor Randolph's pleading face. She would never have thought he could change so much. Looking back, she realized a thing she'd pushed away from her for a long time: Taylor had not been fully to blame. She had flirted with him, encouraged him, finally even announced she would marry him. While he was responsible for his actions with the slave girls, she had been at fault for leading him on.

Dr. Stuart's clear eyes had seen through her — and she had hated it. A vision of herself, neck and white shoulders gleaming, rose to accuse her. Her wearing her dress cut just a bit higher was no excuse. She had seen men's eyes fixed on her, had known a thrill when something dangerous leaped into those watching eyes. She shuddered. Slowly the things of the past had caught up to her.

"I am unclean," she cried out, "O God, can I ever feel clean again?" The walls of the white room pressed in on her, leaving her even more miserable.

Like a breeze of fresh air came Mrs. Stuart's voice, "God gave His own Son to save you and me and all the world." Silver had heard the same thing many times since she came to Harmony. Suddenly it became real.

"I'm too tired to fight anymore God," she confessed. "I still don't understand how You can leave Your world in such a mess, but I can't stand any more. I'm not worth much, but whatever I am, it's Yours. Please," the words flittered on her lips, "forgive me and make me free." She remembered what the Stuarts always said in their evening prayers. "For Jesus' sake and in His name, Amen."

Her torment gradually stilled. In its place

came things she hadn't noticed for weeks: the singing of birds outside her windows, splitting their throats with praise; the smell of honeysuckle and wild roses wafting through the open glass; the sounds and smells of a farm, Iroquois neighing, and a chicken scratching.

She awoke hours later, filled with wonder. Where were the anxieties, the fears that had flooded her? Her fingers shook a bit as she dressed, not in a uniform. Zach had told her to stay away from the hospital. Fresh in the little yellow sprigged-muslin she loved, she stepped into late afternoon. Slanting sunlight vied with the light in her dark eyes. Her hair had grown during the winter months and fell to her neck, atop the fine lace collar. She curled in a big chair on the porch and gazed across the rolling fields, so like her fields at Silver Birches, yet a little more wooded.

Zach found her there when he trod heavily home. There was nothing more to be done for a time at the hospital, and the overpowering urge to get free of all the bloody work and misery of the hospital had been irresistible. He could have ridden; he chose to walk. When he stepped onto the porch and saw Silver there in her yellow dress, his heart lifted. The green eyes grew soft.

Silver looked up and saw him. Color stole through her too-white cheeks, made so by long hours of hard work. Her strong, callused fingers folded themselves tightly together. "Welcome home." An overwhelming desire to cradle his tired head in her lap gave way to shattering enlightenment. She loved him. She loved everything about him, from fiery hair now turned copper in the setting sun to emerald eyes and mobile mouth.

The knowledge left her weak. If only she could spend the rest of her life being there, waiting to cry, "Welcome home!" Her long-ago memory of the look in her mother's face when her father came in filled her eyes with the truth.

Zachary Stuart inhaled sharply.

She knew he had discovered her feelings. It didn't matter. As his lips curved in a tender smile, joy burst inside her, mingled with the peace she had gained earlier, and made her want to dance and sing and shout.

"I'll get into other clothes." His words were a promise. Weariness gone, he bounded up the stairs. Silver sat still and waited, as she knew now she had waited all her life. He had come. Her mate. Her companion.

"Silver and I are going for a walk, Mother."

She caught the lilt in his voice and Mrs. Stuart's, "You have about an hour before supper."

West Virginia had never been more beautiful. The sun had left a rearguard of rosy clouds that sprinkled through the trees and touched their faces. Zach drew Silver's arm in his own and carefully led the way across the pinkened fields. In a small stand of trees was a large stump. He spread his handkerchief, then lifted Silver to it.

"Why, Zach!" But even her laughing surprise at his quick action couldn't conceal her pleasure.

The green eyes looked straight into hers. "Silver, more than a year ago I told you how I felt. I haven't changed."

Could a person's heart burst with sheer happiness? Silver reached out one hand. He caught it easily, turning it over and examining the hard-won calluses, badges of service.

"Such a hard-working little hand. But far more beautiful than ever before." He was deadly serious. "I want that hand, Silver. I also want your heart. I love you the way my father loved my mother. Can you ever learn to care for me in that way?"

She could not give in without a final spurt of independence. She lowered her lashes until they made half moons, dark against the flushed cheeks that rivaled the sky. "No, I can never learn to care that way."

He dropped her hand, stepped back. "Forgive me." His voice was not quite steady. "I thought —"

"I can never learn to care," she went on calmly, in spite of her racing heart, "because I already do." She raised her dark eyes and looked full in his face. Anything else she might have said was smothered in his shirtfront as iron arms seized her, dragged her from the stump, and held her fast. A moment later his lips found hers, not as Taylor Randolph's had once done, but in a kiss that set her tingling, yet held respect for her.

"I love you, Zach." Her quiet words didn't even reach the curious squirrel who stopped on his way home to observe them, but they reached the ears of the man who loved her and whose arms tightened protectively.

I will never be afraid, so long as I have Zach, was her last thought as he kissed her again, this time holding her as if he would never let her go.

They walked home through the twilight, all thought of supper forgotten. Silver had told him, "I told God today I was His," and had seen a kind of glory fill Zach's face. They had dreamed their dreams and made their plans. Zach insisted on not getting married until the terrible war was ended. "I can't be distracted in my work," he warned, and she flamed red at the look in his eyes.

"Then I'll wait and work with you," she promised.

It was not to be. As summer gave way to fall, then winter, Silver could see the change coming over her beloved. It showed in the haggardness of face that was not just from overwork. It betrayed itself even when they were alone and she was in his arms. The day came when Silver could stand it no more. "Zach, tell me. What is it?"

His lips tightened. Sadness such as she had never seen before crept into his face. "I have made a decision, Silver."

Her ability to sense trouble flared.

"I've thought all this time I could stay here, care for those who needed me. I can't. I never thought I would join the army, but if this war is to end, the Union needs every man it can get. I'm leaving at the end of the week."

Silver could not have been more paralyzed if he had struck her. "You're goin' to fight against Virginia?"

"I have no choice."

How many more times would she hear those words? Silver wondered dully. Her lips quivered. "What about your commitment to savin' lives?"

"I will never fire a rifle. I will be on the battlefield to care for those even on the front lines."

His drawn face touched her. "What about your work here?" She bit her lip to keep from crying out.

"You can carry on, with old Doc Harper's help." He took her hands in a grip that hurt. "Can you do it for me, Silver?"

"Yes." There was no question of trying to sway him. He would do what he thought right. It was one of the reasons she loved him. "But oh, come back soon!" Her piteous cry whitened his already-pale face, and he could only hold her heaving body against him for comfort.

13

There were no flags waving when Zachary Stuart rode away to serve the Union, no marching men or shouts of "Whip 'em good!" Just a white-faced girl turned woman, who struggled to hold back tears and refrain from boldly holding him and refusing to let him go. Zach's last sight of Silver was the trembling smile she summoned for his benefit and a scrap of white handkerchief waving through the gloomy morning.

Zach rode without illusion. There would be no glory. He had been beaten with this fact by the hordes of soldiers he cared for in a Harmony that no longer lived up to its name. His face was grim. There was a job to be done, that was all. In all probability he wouldn't be back. Field hospitals, with their rude furnishings, could be hit by cannon fire, as well as enemy ranks. He shuddered. To die in a war that should never have been started! Bitterness crept into his very soul. Back in Harmony lay everything on earth he wanted — Silver, home, and family. Ahead lay hell. On a hill miles out of town he hesitated. Was he insane to deliberately go? It wasn't too late to turn back. God knew there was plenty of need in Harmony. Why not go home and continue the weary rounds he knew so well?

"I can't." Defeat rode his shoulders like a heavy coat, pressing him down. The sleety day turned darker, and the gloom ahead swallowed up and obscured the path he must travel. "God, ride with me. I will never take life, even to save my own."

A single instant he remained motionless, a determined statue etched against the growing storm. A tiny thrust of peace stole into his heart. If God was with Him, all the powers of Satan and war could not withstand that.

It was all that kept Zach going that terrible winter. He lost track of what battle was being fought. Always establishing field hospitals and making use of the most primitive situations kept him busy. There was little time to sleep, much less to think of anything except the terrible need.

One night, strangely silent except for the low moans of patients in lengths of cots stretching on three sides of him, Zach wrote to Silver by the dim light of a carefully shaded lamp.

My darling,
  You will never know what your letters mean to me. Three caught up with me

today. As I read them I could see you in our home, lamplight catching your dark hair, as you bend over the paper writing. Keep sending letters, even when you don't hear from me. My heart cries out even when my hands and mind must be occupied with the wounded — and the sick.

There is no way I can tell you what it's like. Soldiers are dirty and sick and dying. It is the same in all the areas of battle. There are as many — or more — dying from dysentery and typhoid fever and tetanus as from actual combat! Cleanliness is next to impossible in such crude conditions. We are always short of medicine. Sometimes there is little food. I will say this: Never have I seen men such as these. Both northerners and southerners appreciate what I do for them more than can ever be expressed. I have seen starving men sneak a bit of their food into a comrade's rations. I have seen a man leap in front of another and take the ball intended for him.

Strangest of all, I have found that even though I know God hates war, He is here with us. Silver, dearest, when men come to facing death or cannons and rifles, all the questions about God seem to disappear the way the early morning Virginia mists dissolve when the sun rises. Everyone knows my beliefs. Dozens have asked for me on their deathbeds, and even greater than the physical ministry I give is the spiritual comfort I am offering. I never told you how I agonized over my decision, although I know you guessed. I even hesitated outside Harmony that day that seems to have slipped into the shadows of the past.

Now I know. Chaplains are few. I am needed here to witness of the Lord Jesus Christ. Fighting for one's country is not enough — as some of the men believe — there is a Higher Commander.

So even though I hate everything about this war, I cannot help telling you, Silver, I am glad I came. It is what He would have done.

My love,
Zach

"Beggin' yore pardon, Doc, but a new shipment's comin' in." The dark face of Zach's Negro orderly was lightened with fatigue. "The major says at least a hundred."

"God, where will we put them?" It was

not a curse but a prayer.

"I reckon we better move out some of the one's we got now."

Zach's lips set. "We have no choice. George, follow me." His red hair caught the light from the lamp George lifted, and Zach impatiently brushed it back. They marched between rows of cots, and Zach reluctantly roused several of the wounded men. "Boys, we've got others on their way in who are badly hurt." His throat clogged. "Any of you who can give up your cots?"

The man in him cried and the doctor protested as they rose almost to a man. "No, not you, Reyburn. You've earned that cot." He pressed the struggling eighteen-year-old back. "Simpson, stay put." Down the line he went, forcing some to lie back down. George helped the others, the lame, halt, and blind, make their uneven way out of the hospital tent and to shelter nearby.

Then it began, the seemingly endless procession of the new wave of patients. Some needed only a bandage. George did those, assisted by a few ambulatory patients who insisted on remaining to help. Hours fled, and an uneasy dawn broke, heralding another day of fighting. It was good he'd written Silver the night before. The gray-faced major ordered evacuation of the field hospital and moving of the men before noon. Enemy fire was getting closer, and there weren't enough troops to repel it.

Relocation was always agony for Zach, seeing the set faces and bloody lips of men who sank their teeth in hard to keep from "showing yellow" and crying out. Some were too weak and died on the way. Others hobbled, because there weren't enough carts. Zach simply cared for the most badly wounded and shut his mind to all else. When rifle fire and whistling balls threatened, he ignored them.

Days became weeks. Rest became a thing snatched in moments. Zach laughed grimly at the large amount of trouser material he could bunch up around a waist shrunken with too much work, too little food. The superb strength given from God and carefully nurtured by hard work and clean living was being undermined by continuous abuse. When George insisted the Doc sleep, Zach shook his head. "Later." Even when he closed his eyes, the sights, sounds, and smell of war were never far enough away to let him really rest. It wasn't until the day he was performing just one more of a countless number of emergency surgeries and fell asleep on his feet that he gave in. George had caught him as he swayed. Zach straightened, finished his task, and lurched to an empty cot. Blackness covered him.

When he awoke, every bone in his body ached, but for the first time in months he felt totally alert, rested.

"You done slep' thirt'-six hours." George's white grin greeted him.

"You grinning traitor. Why didn't you wake me?" Zach stretched, groaned, and slowly stood up.

The dark eyes rolled. "No, sir! Major says let you be." He held out a tin cup of coffee and a tin plate with bread and stew. "Rations done come in.

Zach ate, feeling strength flow back into his body. "How're the patients?"

"Jest the same."

Zach sighed. It was time to start his weary rounds again. But by midnight, everyone was quiet. He could write Silver again, the first time since that night weeks before moving.

Dearest,

A few lines while the men are sleeping. I have just slept and eaten and am practically a new man. Silver, this is the saddest war that has ever been fought. I saw something a few days ago that is indelibly printed on my mind. I hope you don't mind the reality I tell — just thinking how it might be could conjure up worse scenes for you than are actually here, if that's possible.

It seems a hundred years ago, in the Silver Birches ballroom, when I tried to warn this war would set brother against brother. I've dreaded seeing it happen. I've prayed I'd never come against families shattered by each other. Now it has happened.

The stretcher bearers brought in the wounded. Some wore gray, the others blue. Injury knows no color lines. I was drawn to two of them — one a Yankee, the other a rebel. They resembled each other and looked familiar! I cared for them, and one said, "Did Sam get it?" and held out a torn hand from a blue sleeve.

Then I remembered. I looked at the boy next to him, whose gray coat had been cut away. He opened his eyes and said, "Joe?" They were the same eyes that had laughed a week ago when after the day's fighting was done, the southerners came across the line and played cards and smoked and swapped stories together! I learned then and again later they were first cousins, fighting against each other. Now they lay mortally wounded.

"Sam, why're we here, anyway?" the Yankee whispered. His question seemed to echo through the entire hospital tent. I waited for the answer, as every man within hearing distance did. It's the question I've seen tremble, unasked, on a thousand mouths, in a thousand eyes. Now it was spoken by a dying man.

"Why, Sam?" Joe raised a feverish head.

"I don't know." Sam stared into his cousin's face. "We never fought before. Always stuck up for each other." Already the glaze of death was coating his eyes. "Joe, let's you an' me go home and get the coon dogs out." He gritted his teeth and reached a hand across the small space between them.

The blue sleeve never hesitated. It shot out to meet the hand halfway. "I reckon we'd better."

I thought I was going to die from the pain inside. Before I could move toward them, Sam fell back to the cot, still holding Joe's hand. Five minutes later, Joe died, hand locked in a death grip. I had to pry their fingers apart. We buried them side by side and marked the spot. Later they can be sent home — and "home" for them is the same little Kentucky town.

God forgive whoever it is who starts and maintains the machine of destruction that claims victims. There's a certain expectation of glory when boys and men march off to the beat of drums. But after the drums comes anguish.

I haven't had a letter from you for weeks. I suppose they can't keep up with all our movements. There are times I wonder if your love is all part of a dream, if it never really happened. Then I tell myself God would not allow such a cruel joke and go back to my work, as I must do now.

My love,
Zach

Another time he wrote:

I couldn't stand what is happening, if it weren't for God. Just when I think if I see one more rotting wound or have to amputate one more arm, I'll go stark, raving mad, I remember how Jesus faced leprosy, demons, and the cross, and I can go on.

Nights are the easiest and the worst. The men are usually quieter then, but just before dawn, the spirit is at its lowest. Someday doctors far more gifted than I will discover why. I only know I close more eyes in death then than any other time.

They say relief is on its way. I pray it comes soon. So many of us are ragged and heartsick, we aren't much good anymore. Yet we're bound together by heroism that will never be rewarded with medals, that will never be written up in papers for others to exclaim over. It is the heroism of simply staying alive in hopes of getting home. I never knew the meaning of the word until I came to war.

Hundreds of miles away, winter crept by for Silver and the Stuarts on leaden feet. Letters were read and reread. Silver's heart ached at the conditions Zach and his comrades faced. Every light snowfall brought heartrending questions: Did he have shelter? Was he warm? Or had he given away the heavy coat he had started out wearing?

The one thing it did do was give Silver strength to go on with her daily rounds of the overcrowded hospital. Without Zach, there had been danger of its falling apart. Silver, to her own amazement, stepped in, set up a rude schedule for the volunteer nurses, saved poor old crippled Doc Harper's time for the critical, and saw it was carried out. If there was a gap, she filled it uncomplainingly. She even began whispering a prayer at the bedside of whatever patient she tended.

Despite the hardship, sickness, and worry, once Silver accepted command from her Master, she never wavered. Many times she literally prayed for strength to get through the coming hours. Always it was there. Mrs. Stuart noted the hollow eyes and thin cheeks, but instead of protesting, she took down the old Bible that had come to mean so much in Silver's life, turned the yellowed pages and read, "Then shall the righteous answer him, saying, 'Lord, when saw we thee an hungered, and fed thee? or thirsty, and gave thee drink? When saw we thee a stranger, and took thee in? or naked, and clothed thee? Or when saw we thee sick, or in prison, and came unto thee?'

" 'And the King shall answer and say unto them, 'Verily I say unto you, Inasmuch as ye have done it unto one of the least of these my brethren, ye have done it unto me.' "

Silver's eyes were wet, and Mrs. Stuart stroked the dark head with a compassionate hand. "Child, you will never be given that which is above your strength to bear, if you will trust Him." It carried through into Silver's darkest hours.

After General Lee was defeated at Antietam, called the bloodiest battle of the war, he established himself on the high bluff overlooking Fredericksburg. In an ensuing battle, 5,300 Confederate soldiers were killed and nearly 13,000 Union soldiers. General Ambrose Burnside, on the opposite side of the Rappahannock River, attacked. After six assaults had been beaten off, he withdrew. But the South no longer rejoiced over battles won. They had settled down to the inevitability of a long and costly fight. Back against the wall, the South fought for home, family, a way of life, while the Union fought to preserve itself.

Silver lost track of all the battles. It was enough keeping her own battles won. Troops had gone through and taken much of the food. She often carried in supplies from the as-yet-untouched Stuart place to feed the wounded. Once in a while she caught a glimpse of a gaunt woman in gray gown and white apron and wondered if it could really be Silver Trevelyan. The girl

Silver would have thrown up her hands in horror at sight of uncared-for nails, dark, circled eyes, and unsmiling mouth. The woman Silver merely smiled. It was she Zachary Stuart loved, not the butterfly who had vanished in the mists of the past.

Over two years had passed since her birthday ball. Her twenty-third birthday came and went, marked only by a vase of wildflowers one of her convalescing patients found huddled outside the hospital walls and a rousing cheer from the men she cared for. Strange, it meant more than all the celebrations she had known when she was feted and praised!

What little quiet time she had was spent in the woods near the Stuart farm. The old stump was a talisman, a place she could go to feel close to Zach — and to God. Sometimes she wondered at herself. How could she have lived so many years with God being of no more importance in her life than an interruption at a ball to please her crusty grandfather? Now only her growing knowledge He had indeed given her, a legacy greater than even Silver Birches, gave meaning to her treadmill existence.

One translucent evening she sat on the stump, a crumpled message in one hand. Frank and Lucy Anne had a son. Unaccustomed envy filled her and memory of the strange feelings that had stirred when she stayed awake and held Lucy Anne on their trip to freedom. Someday she, too, would have a son, a miniature Zach. Perhaps a daughter, a replica of herself. There would be a difference. She would teach them from babyhood their need for God and His unbelievable gift of His Son. Their legacy would be above any earthly lands and houses, above hatred for the North or South, even as she had learned. God was not a southern gentleman. He was not a Union sympathizer or a Yankee. He was simply the Heavenly Father who loved all people unconditionally. If she gave no more of a legacy to her children than that, it would be enough.

If only Zach would come home! Tears glittered. It had been weeks since they'd had any word of him. He was in the thickest battles, caring for those who needed, the "least of these."

"I wouldn't have it any other way." Silver spoke aloud and was startled by the quiet acceptance in her voice. "He was right, that night at Silver Birches. He is a Christian, an American, and a Virginian, but most of all a man." How wonderful that he loved her! What a father he would make. She could close her tired eyes and see him striding up the lane, a toddler clutching his pant legs, a baby perched on his shoulder, smiling as she ran to him.

The vision faded. She opened her eyes. She must go home, eat, and get back to her post. One of the nurses was sick, and Silver would take her place.

She slid from the stump, smoothed the worn yellow gown she couldn't bear to part with, and stepped into the lane. She took one step, lifted her face to the sky, and breathed a prayer, highlighted in the after-glow of day.

Strength to go on rushed through her. Before morning her body would clamor for rest she dared not take time from her duties to seek. But her spirit had been bathed in peace. *She could go on.* She must. There was no one to replace her.

Yet in spite of her hard-won, renewed courage, Silver could not help raising her anguished face to the purple and rose and red sky and crying into the heavens above her, "How long, Lord? How long?" before trudging back down the lane that stretched endlessly in her mind, to a faraway field hospital where the man she loved toiled to rebuild bodies torn down by a senseless war.

14

Silver Trevelyan's cry, "How long, Lord," echoed and reechoed across a rended nation. What Zach had referred to as "after the drums" haunted both North and South. Nowhere was it more apparent than in the rude surroundings Zach lost count of inhabiting. War for him had become a monstrous, unending round. Only the knowledge of the good he was doing kept him sane.

Others were not so fortunate. Zach cared for those no more than sixteen or seventeen, whose eyes faithfully reproduced the horrors they had seen. Boys who had dawdled lazy afternoons away fishing or hunting or visiting friends were rudely awakened by war. Some retreated into themselves, refusing to come back to the supposedly "real" world where all that remained were twitching bodies that had once been comrades. Those were the ones Zach pitied most. If only he had more time to talk with them!

He didn't. They were released from his care when their physical condition improved. Most were sent home. In familiar surroundings perhaps the shock would wear off, and they could regain sanity. Zach shook his head. Too many of them would find nothing familiar when they reached home. War had no respect for property. Blackened, mutilated specters of what had been happy homes stood to remind all who passed by the grim reaper had preceded them.

One misty evening Zach received word from George, who was a tired shadow of himself, "Orders we're movin' again."

Forward. Backward. Never enough time to allow men to heal. This time at least his field hospital was nearly empty. Most of the patients had been transferred to better facilities, beyond the sounds of battle, or were back fighting. One wagon could take the few remaining.

Zach wasn't even sure which direction they would travel. After seeing to the comfort of the patients as best he could, he sagged against the jolting wagon box and dozed uneasily.

Minutes or hours or years later, he awakened.

"Halt!" a faceless rider ordered.

George pulled on the reins. A lantern flared, and Zach saw the light glint on a rifle barrel. "Who goes there?" The drawling words betrayed the speaker was a southerner.

One of the patients groaned, and the rifle swung toward the sound. "What's that?"

Freed from his stupor brought on by exhaustion, Zach leaped to the ground and faced the young corporal. "We're on our way to a safety zone. I'm Doctor Zachary Stuart, and. . . ."

"A doc, you say?" The drawl gathered pace. This time the rifle barrel turned toward George. "You, boy. Turn this wagon an' follow us."

"Do as he says, George." Zach climbed back into the wagon box, then changed his mind. "Corporal," he stepped back out. "Take me to your commanding officer immediately. I assume we are prisoners. These men are hurt and will need a place to be cared for when we get wherever you're taking us."

The young corporal blinked at the authority in his prisoner's voice then waved another rider up. "Hawkins, give the doc your horse an' climb in the wagon."

A muttered curse from Hawkins was interrupted by, "That's an order!" Still grumbling, Hawkins did as he was told. The lantern light showed a swarthy face and dark, matted beard in a thin face, young-old, as so many Zach saw now.

Zach mounted to the still-warm saddle,

mind whirling. Prisoners of war. What now? There had been stories from both sides. Some had been treated well. Others — in spite of his courage, Zach felt cold chills playing tag up his spine. He was a doctor and would probably be accorded some consideration. What of his patients? They were too weak to survive in a jail, without proper food and medical attention. Then there was George. A rush of pure love washed through Zach. The Negro orderly had become his brother as they worked together for others. Somewhere deep inside the thought rang a tiny bell. Was that what it was all about, after all?

Zach didn't have time to meditate. The trail they were following had branches hanging over it until he felt he rode through a green tunnel. The wagon creaked and protested at the narrow, cleared path. An eternity later the thickets thinned, and Zach saw the light of campfires ahead.

"Cap'n," the corporal shouted to a tall figure near a fire. "The boys an' me got ourselves some prisoners. An' a doc."

The gaunt man turned. Zach could see the lines of war in his etched face, but he didn't speak.

Zach swung from the saddle and approached. "Doctor Zachary Stuart, sir. I need a place for my wounded."

"Show him a tent. Then bring him back when he gets the prisoners settled." There was nothing in the order to tell whether the captain cared whether they lived or died. No kindness. No harshness. Just words. Zach pondered them as he made his men as easy as rude cots and sparse blankets could do. Lucky it was spring. The bitter coldness of winter was missing, at least.

"What'll they do with us?"

Zach's gaze met George's troubled eyes. He had to be honest. "I don't know."

He was not long in finding out. He'd barely settled his last patient when Hawkins tapped him on the shoulder. "Cap'n wants you."

The campfires threw grotesque shadows in the night as the rebel captain motioned Zach to a seat. An upended packing box served as desk for the writing materials before him.

"Where are you from?" Steely eyes bored into Zach.

"Virginia, the western part."

"Stuart. Seem's I've heard the name. You say you're a doc?"

"Yes."

"Ever carry a rifle against the South?" There was a peculiar note, impossible for Zach to identify, in the captain's voice.

"Never!" Zach spat out the word, the way

he had so long ago at Silver Birches. "Almighty God gave me the skill to save lives, not take them."

"Never killed a man?"

Zach could feel his face go colorless. Why were these particular questions being asked? "Not unless being unable to save lives of those too far gone when I got them and didn't have medicine and instruments available count."

"Hmmm."

Zach couldn't tell whether he was believed or not. The scratch of the captain's pen sounded loud in Zach's ears.

The strange inquisition went on. "Ever save a Johnny Reb's life?"

"Yes."

"More than one?"

"Yes."

"What happened to them after?"

With sickening finality Zach knew why this line of questioning had been used. But he could not lie. "They were sent away."

"To prison?"

"Yes." The word hung between them.

"Far's you know, they all are still alive?"

Zach stared. That same peculiar note had returned to the captain's question. What was he getting at?

"Well?" It cracked like rifle fire.

He looked square into the captain's face, seeing the terrible question in the tormented eyes. "Yes, Captain, as far as I know, they are all still alive."

In the heartbeat before his captor lowered his gaze back to the paper he was using, Zach saw into his soul.

"That's all. We'll know in a few days what'll become of you." As if in answer to Zach's compelling, unspoken question, the captain added, eyes still on his paper, voice gruff. "We need prison doctors — bad."

Zach stumbled back to his men. Prison! The stench he knew was there rose around him, filling his nostrils, in spite of the sweet spring night. Had he been wrong in not bearing arms? At least he would have had a chance to defend himself. There was no defense in prison — just stinking, diseased, dying men, with no escape but death.

News of Zach's capture raced toward Harmony on malevolent wings, striking a fear into Silver that could not be put aside even in her deepest prayers. The Stuarts aged overnight. Only the faith in God the three shared remained. Having each other kept them going each tremulous day. Once Dad Stuart said, "You're our own, Silver." His lips quivered. It hurt Silver to see such a strong man so nearly beaten. "We still have a daughter."

She could do nothing but nod.

Her work increased. There wasn't much time to visit her favorite trysting place, the old stump down the lane. When she did, voices from the past whispered secrets too painfully sweet to bear. Yet between waves of injured, there came a calm. Then old Dr. Harper sent her home. "You'll be no good when the next batch comes," he barked, ignoring how weak his own hands were from lack of rest. "Go home and don't come back until I send for you."

Protest rose to her lips, but she was too tired to utter it. She meekly turned away, never seeing the tears in her friend's saddened eyes or the reflection of herself as she now was — tried by fire and found acceptable, but with youth gone.

It was early summer. The world shouted loveliness, and Silver's heart cried for her mate. Everywhere she looked there were two. Always pairs. Birds. Rabbits. Squirrels. Only she was alone. Even the Stuarts had each other.

Too restless to sleep, she turned Iroquois toward the big stump and let him pick his way. She ought to get out of her hospital clothes and into something clean. Yet the old stump offered more than a fresh gown.

It was her lowest ebb. She slid from her pony's back to the needle-carpeted ground. There had been no more word of Zach. For the first time she accepted the terrible truth: He wouldn't be back. If he had been in prison or even captured, some message would have been sent. There had been nothing. It could only mean one thing.

"No, no!" She rocked back and forth, arms hugging her knees beneath the stained gray gown, rocking back and forth, back and forth, as she had seen other women do when facing the death of loved ones. She could not cry. If she could, perhaps the end-of-the-world feeling would go away. All her tears had been used up for others. There were none left, now that she needed them.

"Silver."

Her nerves twanged. Dr. Harper had been right. She couldn't go on as she was. She was beginning to hear voices calling her from a place she couldn't go yet.

It came again. "Silver."

Her heart leaped. Her head jerked up. Her eyes fastened on the lane before her — and she turned to stone.

Zachary Stuart stood not fifty feet away.

Had she died after all? No, there would be no tattered uniforms in heaven, no emaciated, gray-faced men like the one in the lane. Her eyes feasted on the red hair, now white streaked at the temples. The lips that had kissed her were engraved with deep lines, even though they smiled. Only the green eyes were the same, tender, marked by suffering, but plunging into her soul to glow with love.

She slowly rose, noting the empty right sleeve. Had he lost an arm? What did it matter? The war still raged, somewhere. For her it had ended when she opened her eyes to see him there.

The thought broke her free of the cocoon that had held her. She pelted toward him and was caught in his strong left arm. Sobbing against his chest she heard him whisper, "Say it, Silver."

"Welcome home, beloved!" She raised her face for his kiss. His stubbly unshaven face was the most beautiful thing on earth, and she pressed her lips to his, feeling them flame into warmth. His lone, encircling arm was an iron band, inexorably drawing her closer, until at last she knew it was real, not just another daydream born of her longing and hunger for him.

Sometime later she asked, "Your arm? Is it — ?"

"Not gone. I'll regain some use of it." His

eyes softened to the green of the Virginia hills she loved. "A ball shattered my right wrist. A field surgeon's no good without his operating hand." He gently flexed the stiffened fingers beneath the sling, using his left hand. "I'll have to start over."

"How did it happen?" Silver could sense his need to tell her.

"I was on my way to a prison camp with George and the others." A shade dropped over his eyes. "We were attacked. I don't know whether it was a ball from a Yankee or rebel rifle. It doesn't matter. I lay for some time before they found me, unconscious from a crack on the head. When I awoke, I was back in the encampment."

Silver gasped and held her breath.

"They got me to a doctor. He was as overworked as I'd been. He patched me up as best he could, and I stayed there several days. Fever set in. I can honestly say no one on earth could have been kinder, Silver." The green eyes turned emerald beneath involuntary tears that crowded and spilled out. "I knew prison lay ahead and shuddered.

"That night I felt fresh air coming in the tent. I turned and saw a silver blade flashing in the dim light, then a rip appearing in the tent. When it was pitch black outside, I waited until the doctor stepped out, and I slid through the opening. A voice told me to follow him. I did. He led me to a hill outside camp and said, 'You saved my brother once. Now we're even.'

"I will always believe it was the Confederate captain." He didn't explain. "I made use of the darkness and got to my own camp, but I was all in. What the rifle ball failed to do was almost accomplished by sickness."

Silver could stand it no more. "Now you're home. At least for us, the war is over." Tears she had thought used up trembled on her lashes.

"No, Silver." She could see his stern features looking unseeingly into the distance, across hills that vanished before his memories. "So long as there are men fighting and dying, we will never be free." He turned his eyes to hers, as if glad to escape the horrors for a time. "We'll continue in our hospital, caring for the results of war. But until this world turns to God, its Creator, war will not end." He managed a weary smile. "Come, let's go home."

She paused. "Zach, once you said you didn't want to marry me until it was all over. Do you still feel that way?" She didn't give him a chance to answer but rushed on. "It couldn't have been any harder havin' you gone if we'd been married. Then if anythin' had happened, and we aren't even safe here, I might have had someone to remember you by —" She faltered, hot color pouring into her face.

Something of the old, teasing light crept into his steady gaze. "Really, Miss Trevelyan, am I to understand you're *proposing* to me?"

Her own high spirits that would once have risen to his raillery had been tempered with time and travail. Bright drops fell, and she answered simply, "Yes, Zachary, I am."

His laughter vanished, engulfed in a poignant look Silver would cherish forever. Pure, shining love so deep she could swim in it replaced the teasing. "My darling, we'll be married as soon as we can tell our parents and find a minister." He cupped her face in his one strong hand.

The months of strain dissolved beneath his devotion. Silver rested her tangled, dark head on his welcoming shoulder and silently thanked God.